The Greatest Cause of Mia Dubois

Chris Casavant

The Greatest Cause of Mia Dubois, published April, 2022

Editorial and proofreading services: Cath Lauria
Interior layout and cover design: Howard Johnson
Photo Credits: "Green city on earth, World environment and sustainable development concept," MrJub, ID:844905134, iStock.com

 **SDP Publishing**

Published by SDP Publishing, an imprint of SDP Publishing Solutions, LLC.

SDP Publishing
Permissions Department
PO Box 26, East Bridgewater, MA 02333
or email your request to info@SDPPublishing.com.

ISBN-13 (print): 978-1-7378019-5-5
ISBN-13 (e-book): 978-1-7378019-6-2

Library of Congress Control Number: 2022901185

To Rachel, Samantha, and my students,
who need us to definitively deal with
climate change.

Author's Note

Some of this book revolves around a place called East City, Indiana. East City is fictional. It is, however, substantially—though not entirely—based on the very real city of East Chicago, Indiana, which has dealt with significant environmental racism and climate injustice over the years. It is one of many cities in the United States with a large minority population that has had to endure some combination of polluted air, hazardous drinking water, and contaminated soil.

1

The Storm

Chapter

By the time a hurricane reaches us in Plymouth, Massachusetts, it's usually not a hurricane any-more. Meteorologists call them "tropical storms," and we're used to those.

But Reggie was a real hurricane, a fact that became unnervingly clear on that mid-September day, each time some flying object would ricochet off of our house.

First it was a tree branch. Then a bigger one, so big that it had its *own* branches. Finally, a patio chair nearly barged its way through the dining room wall, as if it was angry with my parents for leaving it outside in the storm.

Not long after I woke up that morning, the wind was already blowing in ferocious gusts. I was convinced that the curtains in the living room were actually swaying, even though Dad had made sure to securely close the windows. The power suddenly went out soon after lunch, and for the rest of the afternoon, my main goal was to distract myself enough so that I didn't panic. I can't say I was very successful.

We all tried not to admit it for a while, but we were terrified. Dad remained calm on the outside. Mom, too. She's always been known for her serenity, perhaps a result of her Buddhist upbringing. But I could tell that they were scared, which didn't help with my own anxiety. "Deep breaths, Mia," I reminded myself. "Deep breaths."

We had tried to eat some dinner around five o'clock, but the fear suppressed my hunger. Plus, with no power, we couldn't cook, and we didn't want to open the refrigerator and let out any remaining cool air. So we nibbled on peanut butter sandwiches for a few minutes. The only highlight was when my annoying older brother Nate's phone died and, no longer able to text, he flipped it disgustedly onto the kitchen table.

It was a highlight for me, at least, if not for anyone else.

Sometime around 6:30, while I was on my bed and curled in the fetal position squeezing my furry, stuffed Celtics basketball, Dad called to us.

"Mia! Nate! Come in the living room! We're gonna have a little, uh, family meeting!"

"What?" I shouted in disbelief. "A family meeting? Why?"

"Just get down here!" he said, making it clear it was an order and not a request.

"Oh my God, fine!"

On my way down the stairs, I glanced out the window at a sky that, given the time, was now providing even less daylight than it had throughout that miserable day. Turning my attention to our front yard, I noticed that it was littered with branches and other debris. The strength of the wind was pushing the trees so hard that some appeared to be bent at about a ninety-degree angle. A few houses over, a powerline had become detached and was resting against the curb.

I climbed onto the loveseat next to Mom, pulling my knees into my chest and hugging them for comfort. Dad was across from us on the couch, staring at a bag of pretzels. Nobody spoke at first. We all wore the same look of concern—even Mom. I didn't understand why we had been summoned to the living room, but being with my parents made me feel slightly better.

"Are we gonna be okay, Mom?" I asked her softly.

"We'll be fine, sweetie," she said. But the usual soothing tone was absent from her voice.

"Why did we have to come in here?" demanded Nate, who finally arrived and sat next to Dad.

"Guys, this room is farthest from the big trees," Dad explained as if he was stating the obvious.

But it wasn't obvious; somehow, it had never occurred to me. Trees? *That's* why they wanted us in the living room? Sure, a few branches, but whole trees? The tops of the pine trees in and around our yard were so tall that they looked like they were in the clouds! After hours of keeping me from panicking, Dad had just uttered one sentence that shook me to my core. I could feel the anxiety building in my stomach.

Incredulous, I glared at Dad. "*Trees* are going to come down?" I shrieked.

"It's not likely," Dad said, "but you never—"

And that's when it happened, as if on cue—the loudest noise any of us had ever heard. Or at least it seemed that way. The whole house appeared to shake. I screamed and squeezed Mom's arm, and I could feel tears welling up in my eyes.

"What the heck was that?" Nate yelled. Nate never yelled. It's one reason I found him so annoying. It's like he didn't care enough about anything to yell. Unless, apparently, our house was being attacked by Mother Nature and her falling trees.

Before anyone responded to him, we noticed that the noises of the storm were suddenly louder. It quickly started to feel cooler. And damp. In the house. It felt like we were no longer inside, or that the storm had let itself in.

As it turned out, the second one was true.

We followed the sound into the kitchen, where there was glass on the floor and branches—green pine needles still on them—jutting through the broken window over the kitchen sink. I stared with a mixture of disbelief and terror. Like, *what are you doing in our kitchen?*

"Oh my God!" Mom said, speaking for all of us as she put her hand over her mouth. My few tears were building into a flood. Dad raced to the bathroom window, from which he could better survey the damage outside. The tree, an eighty-foot-tall pine that, until a minute ago, stood in the corner of our backyard, had crashed onto our deck and knocked most of it to pieces. In the process, the top of the tree had shattered the kitchen window.

Rain invaded the kitchen at a seemingly impossible angle. I was getting colder, but I didn't dare run upstairs for a hoodie. Our yard had three other similarly massive pine trees, after all, and neighboring yards housed even more. I briefly considered what could happen if a second tree came down, this time on the roof, while I was upstairs. Then I squeezed my eyes closed as if trying to force that thought out of my brain.

Dad urgently looked at Nate. "Run into the basement and grab Duck Tape and pruning shears from the work table." Nate stood frozen. "Go!" Dad shouted.

"What do pruning shears look like?" Nate's voice shook.

I didn't know whether to yell at Nate or dart into the basement to look for the pruning shears myself. But Mom took charge. "I'll get them!"

Dad started to sweep up the shards of glass while Nate grabbed a couple of towels to try and dry the floor as much as possible. This task was futile since rain continued to soar past them, voiding their cleanup efforts and seemingly mocking them in the process.

I followed Mom into the basement, which smelled disgustingly musty, even more so than normal. "What are we gonna do, Mom?" I choked out through my tears. "We have a tree in our kitchen!" I tried unsuccessfully to take a deep breath. "I'm really scared."

"We'll figure out what to do." Mom was all business as she searched for the tape that was not on the work table. "Our number one goal is to keep you and your brother safe. You know that."

She dug through a drawer and found the needed supplies, so we raced back upstairs. When we returned to the kitchen, I lost my balance and nearly fell on the wet linoleum floor. Dad took the pruners from her and snipped off as much as he could from the branches that had forced their way into our lives. Luckily, most of them were just thin enough to cut.

Dad then grabbed an empty cardboard box from the recycling bin. He flattened it out and taped it over the window to keep out the rain. But everyone knew that wasn't a long-term solution.

Mom and Dad looked at each other worriedly for a moment as they pondered their next move. I hoped they had a plan because I could barely think straight. I just stood there, shivering and wiping tears from my cheeks. Finally, Dad spoke up. "We should go to your parents' house."

Chapter

"Are you sure that's safe?" Mom asked. My grand-parents were normally only a five-minute drive away. But we hadn't tried it in a hurricane before! Dad was insistent. "What other option do we have? They have no trees that threaten their house."

I was suddenly hanging on every word, like it was a climactic scene of a movie, only it was my real, suddenly nightmarish life. Mom seemed to choose her words carefully, probably to avoid upsetting me even more. "But that drive could be tricky right now. Could we just go in the basement?"

I had wondered that too. But our basement was unfinished. There were laundry machines down there, plus a smelly oil tank and unorganized piles of clothes, toys, and other stuff being stored.

"Honey, the basement is a mess," Dad said. "It's dark and damp. We can't spend all night there. We can barely *sit* down there, let alone sleep."

I looked at Dad, whose eyes revealed deep concern, something I had rarely ever seen from him before. "I'll drive carefully," he said. "I promise."

Mom nodded in reluctant consent. I returned to deep breathing.

We all grabbed coats from the hook behind the kitchen door. Mom opened the door, and as soon as we stepped outside, the wind collided with my face and momentarily took my breath away. I sprinted to the car, hunched forward as rain pelted the top of my hood. Out of the corner of my eye, I saw that Mr. and Mrs. Dwyer's basketball hoop across the street had blown down; since their kids were all grown up and moved out, they essentially kept the hoop for me. Now it was on its back in the front yard, the net holding onto the rim for dear life.

This made me sad, but at that moment, safely making it to my grandparents' house held all of my attention.

Dad backed the car out of the driveway as the rain smacked the windshield. He straightened us out and started to accelerate, dodging several branches that had created an obstacle course on our street.

Almost immediately after the car began moving, I noticed that something was wrong next door. A tree had fallen onto the car in our neighbor's driveway. But that wasn't the worst part; the car's light was on. And from about twenty yards away, it appeared that someone was in the car.

"Dad, look at Don's car!" I said.

Mom's eyes widened when she saw. "Honey, stop!" she yelled. Dad slammed on the brakes.

Our elderly neighbor, Don, had lived alone since his wife died about five years earlier. I felt bad for him because I assumed he must be so lonely, but he always seemed upbeat. I would call him Mr. Francis and, with a broad smile, he would fire back, "Call me Don!"

That night, Don's beat-up navy blue Ford sedan, which he rarely drove, was in its customary spot at the top of the driveway. But the front of the car was sandwiched between the driveway and the trunk of a pine tree.

That day had been traumatic enough already. But when I saw Don's car, my heart sank. Was he okay? I mean, if he were okay, he would have gone in the house, right?

"I'm gonna see if he's in there," Dad said. He all but jumped out of the car.

"Please be careful!" Mom urged.

Instinctively and—I can admit—somewhat foolishly, I darted out of the car, slamming the door behind me. "I'm coming with you!" I yelled to Dad.

I could hear my mom pleading with me to stay, but it was too late. I was gone, running through the rain to catch up with Dad. When he saw me, he didn't yell, but he was very serious.

"Mia, stick right with me," he said. "*Do not* leave my side."

"Okay," I said. I thought helping Dad was the right thing to do, but I was shaking with nerves. I was too afraid to look up because I was sure that more trees were being pushed toward their breaking point by the intensity of the wind, and seeing that would only have fueled my anxiety as I speed-walked up Don's driveway, totally exposed.

As we approached the car, I saw a man in the front driver's seat with thin gray hair, mostly bald on top. It was Don. But he didn't seem to notice us.

Dad, holding his left arm by his face to shield it from the driving rain, yanked open the door with his right hand. At that moment, Don seemed to awaken from unconsciousness, but it wasn't clear that he knew where he was or who we were. Broken glass from the windshield was all over the front seat of the car—some pieces were even in his hair and on his maroon Champion sweatshirt. His old flip phone sat on his lap.

Most of the tree had landed on the hood, but in the process, it had caved in the area around the gas and brake pedals. How was anyone going to get him out of the car?

I noticed the top half of a phone charger in the car's console, but before that discovery truly processed in my brain, Dad handed me Don's phone. "Call 911!" he yelled through the wind and rain. He then turned back to Don. "Hang in there, Don! We'll get you out of here!" Don, eyes open but clearly disoriented, did not respond.

I called 911. By then, Nate had arrived to help Dad pull Don out of the car. Don was barely responsive. Dad and Nate tried to move him, but Dad quickly aborted the attempt. "I'm afraid we'll do more damage to his legs if we try to pull him out," he yelled to Nate.

After telling the 911 operator the details and our location, I turned back toward Don. He was in bad shape. I had never seen anything like it before. I was only twelve, and if this were a movie, I probably wouldn't have been allowed to watch it. Too scary. I looked at Dad. "Is he gonna die?" My voice trembled.

Dad stared at Don and frantically asked, "Are you okay, Don?" Don's eyes were slightly open, but he offered no response. Dad put three fingers on the inside of Don's wrist and felt for a pulse. "Stay with us! The ambulance is coming!"

Dad and Nate sat with Don in his car while we

waited for the ambulance. I returned to ours, where Mom joined me in the backseat. She gently pulled my head under her chin, telling me that we had done all we could, and Don would soon be in the hands of people trained in handling emergencies.

I felt like I should cry. Instead, I sat in shock, taking some comfort in Mom's embrace, but mostly replaying the previous fifteen minutes or so in my mind. Was it fifteen minutes? It could have been five. It could have been an hour. Time seemed to have stopped.

I heard the ambulance before it reached us, so I opened the door and got out of the car to see if I could help. The EMTs surveyed the situation quickly before hoisting Don out of his car. They reclined his seat and carefully pulled him toward the back of the car to ensure his legs were safely freed before lifting him out. Meanwhile, I was still standing outside, drenched and constantly sliding my windblown hair off of my face. I had kept Don's phone securely in the pocket of my coat, and I took it out and handed it to the woman who was about to get in the driver's seat.

"It's his," I said. "Can you make sure he gets it?"

"Of course," she said. "Thank you."

The next thing I knew, she had climbed in the ambulance, activated the siren, and sped away. I turned back toward our car and could see that Nate and my parents were shaken. So was I. I couldn't help but wonder if I had just witnessed the death of our neighbor. Even if he lived, who was going to be there for him in the hospital? What would his life be like? So much about my life seemed to be changing on this one day.

Dad drove very cautiously to my grandparents' house. I don't know if that was because of the hurricane or if he was so freaked out by what had just happened. Probably both.

When we got there, the area around Nana and Papa's house was just as dark as our own neighborhood, but the nearest tree was a safe distance from their house. We ran inside and sat down in the candlelit living room, breathing a sigh of relief. I hugged my grandparents like I hadn't seen them in years.

I was relieved to be in a safer house, but it was a tough night. I couldn't sit still. I couldn't focus on what people were saying. Really, I couldn't erase the previous two hours from my mind, which made it nearly impossible to sleep when I finally lay down on the couch in Papa's office just before midnight. I wanted to call my Uncle James in Chicago. He's someone who always understood me and knew exactly what to say to make me feel better. But it was late, and I didn't even have a phone. Instead, I did a lot of staring at the ceiling, fading in and out of sleep until daylight finally slipped through the window blinds.

Chapter

3

I tried not to think about Hurricane Reggie in the days after the storm, but if someone tells you not to think about a hippopotamus in a tutu, what are you going to think about? Exactly. And even when I actually wasn't thinking about it, the pit in my stomach reminded me.

In Plymouth, where I had lived my whole life, the downtown and waterfront areas were a total mess. Trees were down. Power lines, too. Plymouth Rock, which always seemed to be such a huge deal to tourists, was completely submerged in the Atlantic Ocean. Water Street, the busy road that runs along the ocean, was also, perhaps fittingly, underwater.

Dad had returned to the house two days after the storm to patch up the kitchen window, but all he could do was board it up and cover the wood with sheets of plastic. No contractors or handymen were available for a small job like that, I guess. So we stayed at Nana and Papa's house.

A few hours after Dad had sort of fixed our window,

he came into the kitchen as the rest of us shared a bowl of chips and salsa. "I'm going out for a bit," he announced.

"Okay," said Nate, whose response projected something between apathy and obliviousness, typical for him.

But I was more curious, so I followed him outside. "Wait. Where are you going?"

"I just have to, ah, check on something," he said unconvincingly.

"Come on, Dad, where are you *going*? Are you going to see Don?"

He sighed.

"I wanna come," I said.

"I don't think that's a good idea." He was speaking in a very parental tone that I didn't like. I had been thinking about Don a lot, and I couldn't shake the images from that night and the sadness they caused me. I wanted to know if he was okay.

"We don't know what his condition is," Dad continued. "I'd like to see for myself first. Plus, he might have family there."

"Dad," I said, "I was there." My eyes started to moisten a bit, and when a gust of wind forced me to blink, a tear ran a couple of inches down my left cheek. "I already saw what happened to him. I helped. I wanna know how he is."

Dad knew I didn't give up easily. The tear, accidental though it was, seemed to have broken him. He could tell how much this meant to me, and he caved. "Fine," he said. "I'll tell Mom."

I wasn't wearing shoes, so I ran back into the house to grab some socks and my white Chuck Taylor knock-offs. I sat alone on the edge of the living room couch and slid on each ankle-high sock. As I laced up my shoes, hurriedly so Dad didn't change his mind about taking me with him, I heard a woman's voice on the TV. I wasn't really interested in cable news, but I caught some of what she said.

"The bottom line is," this lady said, "we have climate change to thank for these intense storms like Reggie."

Climate change? Climate change was responsible for hurricanes? I was curious to hear more, but I was too rushed, so I ran back outside just as Dad started the car.

A guy at the hospital's information desk directed us to Don's second-floor room, and as we walked down the hall, I started to feel slightly nauseous. I hadn't spent much time in hospitals, but I still associated their smell with illness. We entered Don's room and noticed a familiar-looking woman sitting on the chair next to his bed. Don's eyes were closed.

"Hi," Dad said in a voice barely louder than a whisper. "We're Don's next-door neighbors. I'm Rob Dubois and this is my daughter, Mia. You're Beth, right?"

Right! It was Don's daughter.

"I am. Thank you for coming. He talks about you guys a lot. It's crazy that we haven't seen much of each other in all the years you've lived next door to him."

Dad nodded in agreement. "How is he?"

"He's okay, I think. I mean, he's alive, thank God. He's on a lot of medication."

It was startling to see Don in his hospital bed. An IV bag was positioned to the right of the bed, and he was dressed in a light blue hospital gown. His eyes were closed and he was asleep, but to me, he didn't look peaceful. Whenever I normally saw Don, he was smiling. This time he was expressionless and surrounded by medical equipment. His legs were covered by a white blanket, but poking out the bottom were two sets of toes, each wrapped in a cast.

I found myself tightly hugging Dad's arm.

I wanted to say something to help Beth feel better, but while I searched for the right words, I just kind of froze. Dad tried to comfort her. "I'm so sorry," he said.

Beth, who looked pale and exhausted, nodded. "Thanks," she said. "I'm glad you're here, actually. Were you guys the ones who gave his phone to the EMT? Did you see him that night? They said a family was there with him. I thought it might be you guys. I'm just trying to figure out what happened."

"We were there," Dad said. "We had just started to drive away from our house because we were worried about all the pines around us. As we left, Mia saw one on his car, and we could tell he was in there."

"The nurse told me he had been in his car," Beth said. "I just got here a couple of hours ago. It wasn't safe for me to drive down here yesterday." Beth seemed to fight back tears, probably feeling guilty for not being by her dad's side sooner. She said her brother, her only sibling, lived in Georgia, and he was trying to find the next available flight.

"I'm just confused about why he was in his car during a—" For a second, it seemed like she was going to curse. "During a darn hurricane."

Then I remembered something from the night of the storm. Don's phone charger! So I forced myself to finally speak up. "I think I might know why he was in the car."

That prompted a very interested glance from Beth and a somewhat disbelieving one from Dad.

"Why?" Beth asked.

"Well, his phone was with him, and so was his charger. We had no power. He might have been trying to charge his phone."

I watched as they pondered my answer for a moment.

"That makes sense," Beth said. "He never uses his cell phone, so I'm sure it was dead." Beth appeared somewhat relieved that her dad may have had a legitimate reason for having been out of his house.

Dad told Beth that we would check back on Don in a couple of days. Removing a pen from his pocket, he jotted down his phone number and gave it to Beth in case she needed any help.

"Thank you both so much," Beth said.

"Your dad is so nice," I said. "He always waves to us when we're going to the bus stop, or outside playing basketball."

"I know. He talks about you guys like you're his family. His Plymouth family. You all mean more to him than you probably realize."

That made me happy and somehow sad at the same time.

"We hope he gets better," I said.

Chapter

We had learned the night after the storm that schools would be closed until further notice. We had no idea if that would be a couple of days, a month, or something in between. Finally on Wednesday, four days after Reggie, we got an answer.

I was in my grandparents' driveway with a basketball that morning, working on my ball-handling since they had no hoop. Practicing dribbling a basketball might sound boring, but I actually love it. Because I wasn't even five feet tall, I needed to excel at handling the ball, passing, and playing defense. I had to compensate for my height shortage if I wanted to be any good, and I really wanted to be good. Whenever I became interested in something, anything less than excelling at it would be a disappointment. I'd never decided whether I considered that a good thing about myself or not.

I dribbled the ball through my legs, and then crossed it low in front of my knees, maintaining control so that no defender could poke it away from me in a real game. This also helped to keep my mind off of Don. I had been wondering how he was doing in the hospital.

Then Nate came outside. Unfortunately.

"What are you doing?" he asked.

"What does it *look* like I'm doing?" I snapped.

Nate was early in his sophomore year of high school. We looked a little bit alike, but his hair and skin complexion were a shade lighter than mine. Dad is mostly French, but Mom is half-Cambodian (her name, Sovonnary, means "golden girl"), so our skin was darker than many of our friends', but not by much. An astute observer would notice, I guess, but it was something I almost never thought about. The shape of my eyes more closely resembled Mom's than Nate's did, too.

Nate was a good athlete, but his sports were lacrosse and cross country (which he ran just to stay in shape for lacrosse), so I knew he wasn't coming outside to play basketball with me.

"My friend Sam just texted me," he said, holding up his phone. I hated seeing Nate's phone because it served as a reminder that I didn't have one. That made me even more edgy. What was he even doing out here? I rolled my eyes and was about to resume bouncing my Spalding.

"He says no school until October first," Nate said.

October first? That was like a week and a half! I quickly turned around and glared at him. "How would he even *know* that?"

"His dad is on the school board or something." Nate didn't react to my agitated tone. I guess he was used to it.

"Apparently they're gonna announce it later today," he said.

I dropped the basketball on the driveway, steadied

it with my sneaker, and sat down on it, trying to process the news. I missed school, mainly because I missed my friends—especially Rebecca, Aliya, and Ariana. Nate, however, seemed unfazed by it. Like, he wasn't happy or sad. That's how he reacted to almost everything. He just stood there like an idiot, sipping from a bottle of water, with almost certainly no worthwhile thoughts going through his head.

"Two more weeks of this?" I said. "And we still have no power at home?"

Nate tilted his head back as he drank the last sips of his water. Then he sauntered over to the side of the driveway and tossed the empty bottle into the trash barrel. I briefly considered throwing the ball at his head.

"You know that gets recycled," I said.

"Then take it out of the trash and recycle it," he replied as he walked back in the house.

This was going to be a long two weeks.

"Mia!" Mom and Dad called in unison that evening before dinner.

I had been reading in Papa's office. It had a soft beige couch, and I would sink so far into it that I must have been nearly invisible. I wiggled my way out and hesitantly walked downstairs, wondering if I was guilty of something. Mom and Dad were sitting side by side on the living room sofa.

"Everything okay?" I asked. This had the feeling of a "talk."

Mom nodded and smiled warmly. "Yeah. We just want to talk to you about something."

Uh-oh.

My mind wandered. I had been a little down since the storm. Nate had even called me grumpy at dinner on Tuesday. Were they going to speak to me about that? Did something bad happen to the house? Was Don okay?

Dad spoke first. "As you know, Mia, there's no school for almost two weeks."

Mom picked up the conversation. "Your father and I have been talking. And we think this could be an amazing opportunity for you to go visit your Uncle James in Chicago."

My eyebrows raised, and my jaw dropped. "Really?" I said, feeling a rush of excitement but wondering if there was a catch.

"Yeah," Dad said. "What do you think?"

"Oh my God, of course I'd want to do that! Have you talked to him? Are you sure it's okay?"

"I called him this morning." Dad was Uncle James's older brother by two years. "I asked him what he thought. I think he's almost as excited about it as you seem to be."

Yay! I *loved* my Uncle James! And not just because he's family. We just had a special connection. I always wished I saw more of him, and now I was about to!

"When will I go?" I asked.

"Tomorrow," Mom said. "The Boston and Providence airports haven't reopened yet, but Hartford, Connecticut didn't get hit quite as bad. So there are flights from there."

"I'll fly out with you," Dad said. "Then I'll come back on Friday. Uncle James will fly back with you in a week or so."

I walked over to their couch and hugged them both at the same time, breathing in the smells of Mom's shampoo and Dad's aftershave, two fragrances that had always made me feel happy and safe. "This is amazing! Thank you guys so much! I'm so excited about this."

I stood up. "I'm gonna go pack!"

"Hang on. There's one more thing," Mom said as she reached into her pants pocket.

"This is my old cell phone," she said. "We had it reprogrammed for you this morning. We think it'll be good for you to have one so you can call us, text us, take pictures. It'll make us feel better if you have your own phone."

A phone, too? Had Christmas and my birthday converged into one day of bliss? "Really? Thanks, guys!" It took effort not to jump around like an NBA player who just won a championship.

"We were gonna wait till your birthday," he said. I would be thirteen in January. "Consider this a trial. It's loaded with parental controls. We trust you, but just remember that we own that thing, and we can take it back at any time."

"I know. And I really appreciate it. I won't mess up. I promise."

This was a big deal. Dad worked in sales for a company that sold washers and dryers, and Mom was a reporter for a small daily newspaper called the *Taunton Herald*. I had once heard Mom joke to her friends about how little money reporters got paid. Plus, she had taken a few years off from work after I was born so she could focus on Nate and me. So this trip, plus adding me to the phone bill, could not have been the easiest decision for them. I was so grateful.

"Does Nate know I'm going?"

"Yeah," Dad said.

"Is he mad?"

"No. The high school is still holding fall sports practices, so he has cross country. Plus, I'm not sure he'd even want to go. He's not as close to Uncle James as you are."

"Take some time tonight," Mom said, "and get used to the phone. I know you've used ours before, but just so you're comfortable with it."

Dad laughed. "Please, she already knows more about those things than I do," he said.

"That's not saying much," Mom retorted. "This table knows more about cell phones than you do."

I burst out laughing, and as I all but sprinted back upstairs with excitement, my phone actually rang. I was so startled that I briefly fumbled it in my hands before sliding my finger across the screen to answer the call.

"Hello?" I said, wondering who had my number before I even knew what my number was.

"Mimi!"

"Uncle James!"

"So are you coming to visit?"

"Yes! I can't wait! Mom and Dad just told me!" It sort of occurred to me that I was shouting, but I didn't really care.

"I can't wait, either! We'll have so much fun. We have *so* much to talk about."

"We always have so much to talk about, Uncle James. That's why I love when we hang out."

"Same here. Well, I'm just leaving work, so I gotta go. But I'll see you tomorrow at the airport!"

"Okay, see you then. Bye!"

Phone in hand, I flopped back into the squishy couch. It felt like there were a million thoughts circulating in my head—a million good thoughts.

"Y ou'll never guess who this is," I typed. Then I tapped the little blue arrow and, for the first time, sent a text from my very own phone.

"You're right, and this is creepy, so tell me or leave me alone," came Rebecca's reply.

"I won't leave you alone. Ever. Because you're my best friend."

"Mia?"

"Yes! I have a phone now!"

"That's amazing!"

"I know!"

"So now I can just text you instead of calling your grandparents. Which, by the way, is super awkward. Can we hang out tomorrow?"

"Sorry," I texted back. "I'm leaving for Chicago to visit my uncle for a week. I'm crazy excited!" I ended the text with a GIF of Charlie Brown and Snoopy celebrating.

"I hate you," Rebecca replied.

"Sorry :("

"Have the best time ever. And text me lots of pics."

"I definitely will."

"So we get this extra vacation, and you just ditch me? I see how it is. I guess I'll have to just get some new friends now."

"Whatever. I'll make new friends in Chicago."

"Hate you. Love you."

"Bye!"

Around eight o'clock the next morning, I hoisted my bloated backpack over my shoulders, and the weight of it briefly caused me to wobble before I steadied myself. I carried it into the backseat before wiggling my arms free from the straps, leaving it alongside the carry-on bag that Dad had dragged out for me.

As the car pulled away, I turned back toward the top of the driveway, where Mom and my grandparents were enthusiastically waving to me. I waved back, and as their figures became smaller the farther we drove, the trip became more real in my mind. I was going to Chicago!

I had convinced Dad to leave a little early so we could check in on Don at the hospital. He was sleeping again—or still—when we arrived. Beth wasn't there, but a nurse tended to him in the room.

"How's he doing?" Dad quietly asked the nurse, a young man who looked barely older than Nate.

"I'm not really sure. I just started my shift. His vitals are okay."

"Has he been awake?"

"Yeah. But he hasn't said much."

I noticed a pen and a small notepad on the table beside Don's bed.

"Can I leave him a note?" I asked the nurse.

"Of course!"

I sat in the same chair from which Beth had talked to us a few days earlier. I picked up the pen with my right hand and steadied the paper with my left. I didn't have much time to think before I wrote, but I felt compelled to write *something*, so that he knew people were thinking about him. I wrote:

Hi Don. Hope you're OK. Miss seeing you wave to us in the morning. Hope to see you soon.
Love, Mia.

Then I added a heart.

"So," Dad said soon after we got on I-495, headed northwest. "You must be excited."

His smile revealed that he felt some satisfaction in arranging this wonderful trip for me. I also got the sense that, as eager as I was to get to Chicago, the trip there was a big deal for him too. It's not like we spent a lot of time together these days, just the two of us.

"I'm super excited, Dad," I said. Mom and Dad grumbled sometimes about how I didn't talk to them as much anymore, now that I was getting older. But today, I was very upbeat and in a chatty mood.

So we talked for most of the two-hour drive to the airport. I filled him in on the first few weeks of seventh grade, which friends were in my classes, the first book I had to read for English, and which teachers seemed most likable so far. I also rambled on about all the ways I was trying to improve my basketball game, and how good I expected our team would be in the upcoming season.

Somehow Dad never seemed bored. As he monitored the GPS on his phone to ensure he didn't miss any exits, he kept nodding and occasionally asking follow-up questions. I wasn't quite as close to him as I was to my mom, but I can admit that I enjoyed the father-daughter time that morning.

Just as I finished telling Dad everything about my life—at least, everything I was willing to share with him—he pulled into a parking spot at the airport. Then his phone beeped.

He took it out of his pocket, looked at it, and smiled. Then he handed it to me. "You'll want to see this. It's from Beth."

The message included a picture of Don. His eyes were open! The text read: "He's awake. In a lot of pain. Will probably sleep some more after the nurse gives him more meds. Showed him Mia's beautiful note. He smiled :)"

I smiled too. Partly because Don was doing a little better, but also because I had made him happy.

"Welcome to Chicago, and thank you for flying with us." Those were the exhilarating words I heard before the airplane came to a stop on the runway. I was especially excited to get off the plane because the guy in front of me smelled like some combination of body odor and the fish section at the supermarket.

"Text your mom, Mia," Dad said. "Tell her we've arrived."

My eyes widened. "Yes! I will!" I had momentarily forgotten about the electronic device that I had been craving at least since I started middle school.

When we got to the entrance to our terminal, I had just started to breathe in the smells from the little Starbucks counter when I spotted Uncle James. I dropped my backpack with a thud and raced into his open arms.

"Mimi!" he yelled. "This is crazy! I can't believe you're here!"

"Me either! Thank you soooooo much for this!"

"No, thank *you*. We're gonna have so much fun."

"Hey James." Dad had caught up to us and was patting his brother on the right shoulder. "How are ya?"

"I'm good, Robbie. I hate that it took a big storm for this to happen, but it's nice to see you."

"It's great to see you, too. Mia is as excited as I've ever seen her. Honestly."

I felt a rush of excitement on the walk from the baggage area to Uncle James's car. O'Hare International Airport is huge, like its own town, and taxis and shuttles whizzed all around us while the sound of planes landing and taking off made it impossible for us to hear each other. I had been to Boston several times, and I just loved the sights and sounds of a city. O'Hare was about twenty minutes northwest of where my uncle lived, but the anticipation was building.

Uncle James lived alone on the North Side in a smallish two-bedroom apartment in the Ravenswood neighborhood. He had never married, which always surprised me. I mean, he was a handsome guy and all. He was fun to be with and kind to everyone. Dad once told me that Uncle James was "impossible to please" because he's so passionate about his beliefs, and he seemed to want someone just like him.

"I don't think there's room for two of those under the same roof," Dad had laughed.

Mom had said before that I was a lot like Uncle James. And *I* loved being under the same roof as him. Anyway, the fact that he was single was fine with me because it meant that I would have all of his attention that week.

He lived on a tree-lined street off of Montrose Avenue. His apartment was on the second floor in a V-shaped complex with an open grassy area in the middle. Looking out the car window as he searched for a parking spot, I saw that the nearby streets were quite busy, but this was not downtown Chicago—it was very residential. Up and down these streets, I noticed shops, restaurants, and more apartment buildings. Every few minutes, a train zipped by, making a loud "click-click-click" sound against the metal rails. It sounded like beautiful music to me.

Uncle James's apartment felt very cozy and comfortable. He had lived there for nine years, after all, and had been in Chicago for his whole adult life, since college. His spare bedroom was his office, which would be my room for the next week.

"The couch opens into a bed," he said. "What do you think?"

What did I think? It was perfect! I took it all in—a nice couch, a TV on the wall, and a writing desk. A tall stand-up mirror rested against one of the baby blue walls, which were decorated with framed artwork and photographs.

I fought the urge to scream with joy. "Um, it's perfect. It looks like it's set up for a princess!"

"It *is* set up for a princess," he said with a smile.

That early-fall evening we walked to the nearest Chicago-style pizza place, and we were lucky enough to get a seat right away. As soon as the door opened, the pizza smell made my mouth water. It tasted even better than it smelled, and between all those calories and the travel fatigue, I could barely keep my eyes open on the way home.

The next morning, we brought Dad back to the airport. I gave him a long hug.

"Thanks again for letting me come here," I told him. "It means so much to me."

"You're welcome, sweetie," he said. "Be good to your uncle. And have a blast!"

Chapter

"What do you wanna do today?" Uncle James asked me Friday morning while we munched on French toast at a diner across from his apartment.

"I don't even know where to start," I said. "I don't know much about the city. Only that it's big."

"Museums, theaters, an amazing zoo, an aquarium, endless shopping. Plenty to do. I have to work a little bit today, but I took next week off. So we might have to wait until the weekend to really go crazy."

I knew that he would be working from home a bit during my visit, so I had brought a few books—and my new phone—and was prepared to entertain myself as needed.

"What exactly *is* your job, Uncle James?" I asked him. "Mom and Dad talk about your work sometimes, and I know you help people, but I never really understood what you do."

He held up his index finger while he finished chewing, and then he started to explain. "I work for an organization that helps people in the city who are struggling, or not being treated fairly. Sometimes I'm helping register people to vote. If an apartment building is falling apart, or the people living there are mistreated, I go talk to them, find out what's going on. Then I go to City Hall and advocate for them. Things like that."

"Do you work for the government?"

"No," he laughed. "I'm more likely to bug the heck out of the government until they help us out."

"So who's your boss?"

Uncle James said that many years ago, a rich family started a "nonprofit," which raises money and spends all of it on paying employees and helping poor people in the city. "The founder's son, Avery Carlson, is the one who runs it now. So he's my boss."

"He's rich?"

"Very."

"Does he really care about poor people?"

"He honestly does. His whole family does. They're good people. They chose to do positive things with their money. I respect them for that."

"Cool!" I said.

I looked out the window of the diner, where the sidewalks and streets were filled with people walking, jogging, biking, pushing strollers. Going in and out of coffee shops and bakeries, or waiting for the next bus to arrive. So much to see and do.

"I can't believe you live here," I said with obvious envy.

Uncle James smiled, and then changed gears. "So," he said, "what was the night of the hurricane like? It must have been scary."

"Yeah," I said. "I still can't believe it. I've tried not

to think about things like if the tree had fallen on one of us. I've never been so scared in my life. We were all freaking out. I hope that never happens again."

"Yeah, I certainly hope a tree never falls on your house again, if that's what you mean," he said.

"But the storm," I said. "Mom and Dad say that storms like that are rare where we live. Maybe it won't happen like that ever again. At least in my life."

"Let's hope."

Hmm. I was expecting him to say, "I'm sure it won't, Mimi," but I sensed he was holding something back. "Well, we don't get many hurricanes in Plymouth. Right?"

He seemed to hesitate.

"What, Uncle James?" I insisted. He sighed.

"Have you heard of climate change? Global warming?"

"Yeah. We learned about it in elementary school."

"Storms like that, they're more intense now. It's because of the climate. The weather patterns are getting pretty crazy. Droughts, floods, heatwaves, wildfires, storms. Major storms are becoming more common."

"Wait. That's climate change?" I furrowed my brow and looked at him, perplexed. Then my mind quickly raced back to what I had heard on the news soon after the hurricane. Was that what the lady on TV meant about climate change causing Reggie?

"I thought climate change was about recycling bottles and protecting sea turtles and things like that," I said. "Temperatures getting a little warmer. I didn't know it had anything to do with storms."

"Recycling bottles is a small part of it," he said. "The planet is getting warmer. The climate is changing because we use so many fossil fuels. Gas, oil, and coal. Our cars, planes, electricity—all of it uses fossil fuels and disrupts the climate. We burn the fuels, and the gases stay in the air and trap in heat. And we keep using them. It's like we're determined not to change."

I was stunned by this. Until that moment, I had never heard a single person I know make a big deal about climate change.

"So because we keep driving and using so much electricity, we might get more powerful storms in Plymouth? Is that what you're saying?"

"In a way, yeah. And it's much worse in other parts of the world. The storms that have hit Puerto Rico, Louisiana, Texas—those have been way worse. And parts of some cities and islands are basically getting swallowed up by the ocean now because of sea-level rise."

Huh?

"*Sea-level rise?*"

A few minutes earlier, it had seemed like Uncle James was speaking very carefully, like he hadn't wanted to upset me. But now he wasn't holding back.

"Every year, as we make the planet warmer," he said, "the ice around the North and South Poles melts. There's a huge ice sheet on Greenland and massive glaciers in Antarctica that are at risk. When the ice melts, more water goes into the ocean. That causes the sea levels to rise. If you melt a huge block of ice in a bathtub, what would happen to the level of the water?"

"It would go up."

"Exactly. That's what's happening. Many areas that are nice beaches now probably won't be by the time you're old and gray."

I could feel myself getting angrier with each word Uncle James said.

"At school they tell us to reduce, reuse, recycle," I said. "So I do that. But no one has ever told me that all this crazy stuff is happening. How do you know?"

"Scientists have been studying it. Anyone who has bothered to read about it knows about it. But with most people, I can't tell if they don't care, or if they figure they can't fix it on their own, and since no one else is acting, what's the point?"

Then I thought about my parents and wondered why they hadn't urged Nate and me to pay more attention to this. Actually, why didn't *they* seem to care about it? I had always considered them to be amazing parents. But it suddenly seemed like they had let me down.

"How long have people known about this?" I asked.

"A long time," he said. "But it became national news about thirty years ago. A scientist from NASA told the government about it, and people paid some attention to it. For a while. Then they seemed to lose interest in it. Every few years, a bunch of world leaders get together to talk about it, and they say they will make changes, but then they really don't, and not enough people hold their feet to the fire."

"What? Are people that dumb?"

"Well, nobody has more money than the oil companies. And they've used that money to spread lies, and to basically buy support from people in government. Plus, governments give hundreds of billions of dollars a year to help oil companies. Forget trying to stop them; world leaders actively *help* them."

"Your job." I was now struggling to form sentences. "Do you ever do anything about it?"

"Yes, Mia. That's what I've been working on lately. In fact, I was originally going to a climate rally downtown today until your dad called. We've been working on—"

"Let's go then!" I interjected.

"Huh?"

"Let's go to the rally. Today. When is it?"

"No, I don't think that's the best idea. I told your dad I would take care of you, not bring you to work."

He could tell I was upset. I pleaded with him, "But I want to go, Uncle James. You told me all that stuff. Now I'm mad. I want to go."

He gave it some thought. I stared at him as if trying to persuade him with a Jedi mind trick.

"Okay, but on two conditions. We have to get your parents' permission, and you'll stay with me on the outskirts of this rally. You should see these from a bit of a distance before really jumping in. You're twelve."

"Fine. I'll call him." I ripped out my phone like a gunslinger from the Wild West.

"That's okay," Uncle James said. "I'll call."

Chapter

Dad answered Uncle James's call, and I found myself hanging on every word that I could hear.

"It's a rally about climate change," Uncle James said. After a brief pause, he repeated: "Climate change."

I couldn't hear Dad's voice through the phone, no matter how much I strained.

"Yeah, the rally will be pretty tame, but I promise we'll stay away from the crowds."

Thankfully, Dad didn't mind if I attended the rally, as long as we were "careful." Whatever that meant.

So that afternoon, to get downtown, we took the train, or the L—short for "elevated," Uncle James told me, since most of it is above street level. We got off the train and walked through a few busy intersections, trying to stay with the flow of pedestrian traffic while not getting run over by someone on a bike, or an aggressive cab driver attempting to turn into a sea of people. We finally reached the edge of Millenium Park, the site of the rally. There were a few signs that said it was called "A Rally for Climate Justice."

As we approached the park, the rally had already begun. It was much more laid-back than I expected. A well-dressed man stood on a small black and silver stage, where he spoke calmly to the crowd, which included a hundred or so people standing near the stage and dozens more spread out behind them. This man spoke in a boring way, like one of those teachers whose monotone voice could put you to sleep. But the stuff he said definitely caught my attention as we continued walking and searching for the right spot.

"The world has warmed by about one degree Celsius," Monotone said. "If we don't change our ways, it will get significantly warmer by the end of the century. The consequences would be very dire. We have to make sure the oil companies are stopped before they destroy the planet."

We arrived at an opening on the outskirts of the main crowd, where we could stand and observe the rally. By the end of Monotone's speech, I already had questions.

"What does he mean about the planet warming one degree Celsius?" I asked Uncle James.

"You know how we use Fahrenheit for how hot or cold it is? And most of the world uses Celsius?"

"Kind of."

"Okay. Well, thirty-two degrees Fahrenheit is cold, but thirty-two Celsius is like ninety Fahrenheit."

I stared at him, trying unsuccessfully to do the math in my head.

"Anyway," he went on, "the planet's overall temperature is a bit more than one degree Celsius warmer than it was before we started using coal and oil and driving cars and flying planes. That's almost two degrees Fahrenheit."

"Is that a big deal?" I asked.

"Yeah, that's why these storms are happening more often. The air is warmer, the oceans are warmer. The climate is out of whack." He shook his head in disgust. "And it's because of humans. We're causing so much damage. We think we can do whatever we want and it'll all be fine, like the planet is here to serve us. It's clear now that's not the case."

I stared up at some of the city's skyscrapers, unsure how to react. I had been taught so much during the nearly thirteen years since I was born, but now it all felt like a giant fraud. Somehow the "we're ruining the planet" part was left out.

While the next speaker was being introduced, my eyes scanned the crowd and noticed its various skin colors. It wasn't like Plymouth, where basically everybody's skin was a half-shade lighter than mine. At the rally in Chicago, brown or black skin was common, and while many of the people looked like they were in their twenties, others were as old as my grandparents. A few of them sat in portable camping chairs.

The next speaker was a short Black man with long dreadlocks that had an ombre effect, making them more yellow as they progressed away from his head. He was a much more energetic speaker.

"And it's us, those of us of color, who are paying the most dearly for this," he said. As he spoke, he sometimes rose onto his tippy toes when his voice got louder, and he used his hands a lot. The crowd responded with enthusiastic cheers and applause.

"The hazardous waste, the coal, the lead, all the other chemicals—those aren't in white neighborhoods," he said. "You don't see that in the suburbs. You don't see that on the North Side. We, on the South Side, are the ones dealing with all that! We're the ones suffering from the physical and mental effects of all that. And—I know this will come as a major surprise—nobody is running out there to clean the air we breathe. If they get there at all, they're walking. Backwards. In high heels!"

The crowd roared. I found myself cheering, too, even though I couldn't completely comprehend what he meant. But his passion, and the effect it had on the crowd, gave me chills.

I needed more information.

"What does he mean by that?" I asked Uncle James.

"Pollution is much more common in areas where most of the population is not white," he said. "Has been that way for a long time."

Based on what I had learned in school about racism, I can't say this surprised me. But it definitely ticked me off.

During the next speech, I noticed Uncle James smiling and waving to someone. A woman and her son, who seemed to be about my age, came right over to us. Uncle James hugged the woman and then put his arm around the boy. It was clear that they were all thrilled to see each other.

"Mia lives on the East Coast," Uncle James said as he introduced me to his friend Tracey and her son Hector. "She's out of school because of the hurricane, so I get some time with my favorite niece." I chuckled; he had no other niece.

"And he brought you to a climate justice rally?"

Tracey said with a smile. "He couldn't just spend some quality time with you around the city?"

"I wanted to come," I said. I looked at Uncle James. "He was telling me about how Hurricane Reggie had something to do with climate change."

"Now she's mad, and one thing about Mia—you don't want to get in her way if she's fired up about something."

"That's what I like to hear!" Tracey said. "We'll need you, because for years we've been coming to these rallies, writing letters to all kinds of important people. Nothing really gets done."

"I wouldn't say *nothing*," Uncle James said. "We did get a coal plant shut down on the South Side."

"Really?" I asked. That sounded significant.

Tracey nodded. "Yeah, these rallies have gotten bigger over the years, I will say that."

Until then, Hector hadn't said anything. He was a few inches taller than me, brown skin and black hair. He just looked out at the stage through his dark gray glasses. I couldn't tell if he was shy or just focused on the rally.

"Why are you guys here?" I finally asked him.

"We always come."

"Hector takes this very seriously," Tracey said.

Uncle James and Tracey started chatting, so I decided to strike up a conversation with Hector. I learned that he was eleven years old and from East City, which is in Indiana, just outside of Chicago and the Illinois border. His dad had died a few years earlier after struggling with "health problems," as Hector put it. Tracey worked at an office-supplies store during the day, and a few nights a week, she waited tables at a Chicago pizza restaurant.

"She almost quit the restaurant a few months ago," Hector said.

"Why?"

"My aunt was watching me one night and I had an asthma attack. It was real bad. They say I coulda died."

Hector said that on that June night, while his mother served pizza in downtown Chicago, he was outside playing with some other boys. They were chasing each other and having fun. Suddenly, he found himself gasping for air.

"They thought I was faking so I wouldn't get caught," he recalled.

A teenage girl who was outside with her friends got scared and called 911. One of the boys raced to tell Hector's aunt. An ambulance rushed him to the emergency room. He spent a night in the hospital. Fortunately, he recovered.

"Thank God," I said.

Hector gently patted the cross necklace that was draped over the front of his red Chicago Bulls hoodie. "I do every night."

On the train ride back to the North Side, there were so many questions I wanted to ask Uncle James. But I was mostly intrigued by Hector. His life seemed very different from mine. More difficult.

"I feel bad for Hector," I told Uncle James.

"Why, what did he tell you?" he asked.

"Well, his dad died, which is so sad. And he said he almost died from an asthma attack."

"He's an incredible kid."

He went on to explain that Hector really struggled

in school; reading was difficult for him. He also found it hard to control his temper during moments when he felt overwhelmed. Tracey learned when Hector was in first grade that his blood had elevated lead levels, which can affect the brain of a child.

Then, a year or so later, the government told the residents of Hector's housing complex that the soil all around it was highly contaminated with lead, and that the residents needed to move.

"No one apologized to them or anything," Uncle James said. "It was like, 'Move it or lose it.'"

I didn't get it. It wasn't his fault that they were surrounded by lead, so why didn't the government try to make it better for them? Was it, like the speaker at the rally was saying, because Hector and Tracey weren't white?

"Hector's doctor also thinks that the poor air quality from the city's industries caused his asthma," Uncle James continued. "That's why he goes to a lot of those rallies. It's like he's dedicated his life to this, and he's only eleven. His mother brings him to every one she can. The two of them inspire me. I've picked him up and brought him a few times when she had to work."

"What happened to his dad?" I asked.

"I didn't know him," he said. "I guess he smoked, and he was sick a lot. One winter, he got the flu and his body couldn't fight it off."

I stared at the empty train seat across from me.

"You okay, Mimi?"

"Yeah," I said, not even convincing myself.

"This weekend, we'll do all the fun stuff you want," he said. "And tomorrow morning, we're going to Over Easy. Best breakfast on the North Side."

Of course I knew that I'd have a great week with him. But at that moment, I couldn't shake all that I had learned in the previous few hours. I felt different, even if I couldn't articulate how. There was so much new information in my brain, all of it unsettling.

I felt compelled to do something about climate change. To get involved. To act in some way.

That night, as we had a snack in the kitchen, we could hear the news on the living room TV. Another hurricane had struck, this time causing serious destruction in Florida.

I remembered hearing about the hurricanes that had ravaged Puerto Rico and Houston in recent years. I knew about Superstorm Sandy from when I was very little. And the wildfires that torched California and even Canada in recent years. I never knew that climate change could be to blame for these disasters. No one ever told me that.

What was going on? And did most people even notice? Or care? And if not, *how was that possible?*

Chapter

"This pizza is ridiculous," I said Wednesday night as we wolfed down our dinner at Gino's East. "This is the best one I've had this week. So good. So. Good."

"I told you I was saving the best for last," Uncle James said. "So have you enjoyed Chicago?"

I started to answer, but a pile of cheese and sauce acted as a mute button for my mouth. I washed it down with lemonade so I could speak.

"Yeah, Uncle James, it's been awesome! I love it here. There's so much to do, so much going on all the time. Now I can forgive you for hardly ever visiting us."

Uncle James smiled. He knew I was only kidding.

"Are you ready to go back home on Thursday night?" he asked. "I hear your kitchen window is fixed now."

"Not really," I said. "I mean, I miss everyone. I don't know. I do want to check on Don."

I had received a text from Dad the night before, saying that Don was still in the hospital and struggling.

He had two badly broken legs and would need to be in a wheelchair. I had fought back tears when I read it, just thinking about him, not only alone but now unable to do his normal things. How would he get through his days in a wheelchair?

My visit with Uncle James had been great, as I expected. We went shopping, sat in coffee shops and chatted, visited the Lincoln Park Zoo, and stayed up late to watch "Hoosiers," which instantly became one of my favorite movies. I even learned that Uncle James was a vegetarian who cheats for the holidays.

Still, though, what I had learned about climate change was beginning to seep into all parts of my life. During our city travels, I'd look around and wonder why no one seemed to be preoccupied by the climate problems. People were living their lives like normal. How? Why? The roads were filled with cars. Air conditioners pumped out cool air in the stores, and it wasn't even that hot out. Massive jets soared overhead.

Do these people not know? Do they not care?

"I planned something for tomorrow behind your back," Uncle James told me on the L back to his apartment. "We're going to take Hector and Tracey out to lunch."

"Oh, cool!" I said. "I'd love to see them again."

So the next day, sadly my last in the city, we walked outside to get in the car and drive to East City. Uncle James stopped on the sidewalk, seemingly frozen.

"What's the matter?" I asked. At first I was a bit concerned by his reaction.

"I have no clue where I parked. No clue at all." He

started to chuckle. "This happens sometimes. Wait until you're in your forties."

It was then that I realized we hadn't actually been in the car since dropping off Dad at the airport a week earlier. This was part of what I loved about Chicago—if we decided to go somewhere, we usually walked. Otherwise, we took the train.

"Do you remember where we parked?" Uncle James asked.

I looked directly across the street and laughed. "Uh, it's right there."

He shook his head. "How am I gonna survive when you leave, Mimi?"

More like, how was I going to survive? Who was going to answer all of my questions?

It took us forever to get to East City with all the traffic. But I didn't mind. It gave me a better view of the skyscrapers while we slowly rolled past the downtown area.

As we pulled off the highway, though, I began to notice a change in my surroundings. Suddenly, the buildings looked different. A handful appeared to be abandoned. Fewer trees lined the streets. Uncle James could apparently sense what I was thinking.

"The government kind of neglects people in some places," he said.

I recalled some of what I had heard at the rally the week before. "Neglects them because they're not white?" I asked. My voice dripped with disgust. Uncle James didn't answer. He didn't have to.

When we finally pulled up to the apartment building, Hector and Tracey were all smiles as they walked toward the car.

We ate lunch at a small restaurant outside of town. While the mac and cheese was just okay, the conversation was great. Hector and I found some things we had in common. For example, we both liked to write fiction stories in our free time. Basketball was his favorite sport, too. And we both loved Bruno Mars and Beyonce, as well as some older music—I had become a Beatles fan because my Papa always played their music at his house, while Hector said he was "obsessed" with Marvin Gaye. "Listen to 'Mercy Me,'" he said. "You'll thank me later."

And now, climate change was a shared passion. I knew I was making a friend that day.

To be honest, I found Hector pretty inspiring. I mean, despite his asthma, school struggles, and the area in which he lived, he appeared happy. Or, at least, not angry. His life had been more difficult than I could have imagined. He must have been so strong.

If Hector wasn't angry, I was. As I went to bed that night, I was not only sad that I'd be leaving Chicago the next day, but also frustrated. Frustrated for Hector. For my own future.

And frustrated at my parents.

Chapter

"How come you never told me that the planet is basically burning, and it's our fault?"

Okay, so maybe that wasn't the *best* way to greet my parents on Friday morning, the day after I returned home from Chicago. But I was upset. I felt let down by my own family, the people who were supposed to teach me about my place in the world and prepare me for the future.

It had been late Thursday night when I landed in Boston. I slept for most of the ride home with Dad, and when we arrived, I stumbled through the front door, dragged a toothbrush across my teeth without even opening my eyes, and then collapsed into bed.

When I woke up Friday, I was rested and ready for battle. Mom didn't really appreciate my question, I guess.

"That's quite a response to 'Tell us about your trip, Mia,'" she said.

"We missed you, too," Nate added.

I didn't need to hear from Nate, of all people, and I angrily shot him a look. "Who's even talking to you?"

"Mia, what's going on here?" Dad asked. "We've been looking forward to seeing you. I know you're accusing us of something, but I don't have any idea what it is."

"The planet, Dad. Climate change? The planet's getting warmer because we can't stop driving and flying and using so much electricity. Do you not know about this, or do you not care?"

Mom scowled. "We can talk about this, Mia, but your tone needs to change real fast."

It was clear that Mom was upset, so I tried to dial it back a little, despite my own frustration.

"Fine, Mom. I wanna know why we aren't doing anything about climate change. Don't you care about our future? What if I ever have children? What about their future? I can't believe I had to learn about all this from Uncle James."

"I think I need to have a chat with your Uncle James," Dad said with a smirk that convinced me he was not taking me seriously.

"It's not funny, Dad!"

This cracked up Nate. I furrowed my brow and tried to stare a hole through his annoying face.

"It's not like we don't care," Mom said. "We recycle. And we're not exactly flying to Europe every week."

"Dude, we learned about it in school in like fifth grade," Nate said. "You're acting all surprised about it."

"Oh please," I responded with disgust. "Reduce, reuse, recycle. That's real helpful. So we throw empty bottles in a recycle bin. You don't even do that, moron."

Nate left the room. He had heard enough. That was fine with me.

But then Mom left too. "We can talk about this

when you're prepared to be civil." She followed Nate into the living room.

Now that we were alone, Dad tried to calm me down. "What exactly did Uncle James tell you, sweetie?"

I wasn't ready to be calmed.

"That the planet is getting hotter, and it's causing bigger storms. Like Reggie, which could have killed us, Dad."

We sat together at the kitchen table. I just stared at my half-full bowl of Life cereal. A few tears started to slide down my face, and Dad noticed them, so he leaned over and rubbed my back in a failed attempt to comfort me.

"Dad, the coast of Plymouth might be underwater when I'm old. Ice and glaciers are melting, and it's making the sea level rise. I guess people in some countries have already lost their homes. I just don't understand why this isn't a huge deal in our lives. In everybody's lives. Why does basketball practice matter? Or math class? Or that your company sells another dryer? How come Mom's not writing stories about that for her paper?"

"I don't really know much about sea levels," Dad said. "I hear stuff on the news, but I haven't really paid close attention. I can't imagine Plymouth will be underwater, but I'm sure people can just move away from the ocean. I'm sure there's a plan for this kind of stuff. There's no need for you to worry about it."

"This guy who spoke at the rally I went to, he said the people with money will figure out ways to deal with it, and the poor people will be in trouble," I said. "And I met a kid out there, and him and his mom are pretty poor. Who's gonna help them?"

"Sweetie, I'm sure they have a plan for it," Dad repeated. Maybe he was trying to make me feel better. Or convince himself.

"It doesn't sound like there's a plan," I said. "Ask Uncle James."

So here's the thing about me. I've often been really intense when I've cared a lot about something. I mean, I'm generally a bit shy in school, but once in a while, I become so focused on a task that it's like I've blocked out everything else. Mom and Dad have said it was often a great characteristic, but not always.

I have examples. Like in February, when my basketball team had reached the South Shore twelve-and-under girls' championship game. We were losing by eight points with three minutes left, but from that point on, I scored two baskets, dived on the floor to secure a loose ball, grabbed a rebound around girls way taller than me, and then scored the game-winner on a twelve-foot shot with five seconds left.

"I knew you were good," Rebecca told me as we waited to hear our names during the trophy presentation, "but that was sick!"

But sometimes, the outcome was not as good.

A few times the previous winter, I saw the same homeless man outside of the local supermarket. It bothered me so much. He held a sign that read, "Veteran. Homeless. Any help appreciated." I wanted to help him.

I asked Mom if I could go shopping with her one Saturday, and I brought some money. I handed him five dollars on our way out, and when we got in the car,

Mom said, "Don't give him too much money. He might not spend it on food."

"What do you mean?" I asked.

"I don't know. Sometimes they spend it on drugs. Or alcohol."

I didn't really believe her, so I tried to get my friends and classmates to pitch in.

Some expressed mild interest initially, but after a few days, it was clear that no one shared my commitment. So I got angry with them. I asked them why they wouldn't help more, and they said they didn't want to give away their allowance to some guy on the street.

"But he needs that money way more than you," I'd say.

"What if he's lying?" one of them said. "What if he's just trying to scam us?"

"He's going to sit outside in the cold, in old raggedy clothes, for a few dollars?" I asked rhetorically.

They got tired of hearing about it. And I got tired of them. So I stopped talking to them for a while, and they made no effort to talk to me. I felt bad that my friends were upset with me, but I couldn't understand why they were unwilling to help a homeless man who fought for our country.

When I told Mom about it, she said, "Not everyone is like you, Mia." I still don't know if she meant that as a compliment.

"Don't you owe me an apology?" Mom asked a few hours after our unpleasant morning chat about climate change.

"Don't *you* owe *me* one?" I replied.

I guess Mom thought enough time had passed for everyone to have cooled off. As she usually did once a day, Mom had performed a mindfulness meditation exercise, where she sits on a cushion with her legs crossed and attempts to focus solely on her breath, calmly allowing outside thoughts to pass through her mind. When she goes into her room, closes her door, and puts on calming music, I know that's what she's up to.

She had tried to convince me to start meditating before, but I frustratedly gave up after a few futile attempts to stop my mind from wandering. I have no clue how she does it.

Mom sat down next to me on the living room couch. It was clear this wouldn't be a brief, simple conversation.

"Mia, please explain to me, calmly, exactly why you're so upset."

I was happy to explain. In fact, I needed to talk about it.

"Mom, people are doing awful things to the planet. *We* are doing many of them. Why have you and Dad allowed us to do this stuff? Why haven't you ever told us?"

"What awful things, Mia?"

"Well, driving. Cars use so much gas and oil. It's making the planet hotter. Why do we drive so much?"

"Mia, what do you propose we do? Should I walk to Taunton every day? Take a bike down Route 44?"

I hadn't really thought about that.

"Well, what about all the electricity we use?" I asked. "And oil for our heat? A guy at the rally in Chicago talked about burning fossil fuels for electricity, and how bad it is. He said we need to stop using them."

"Okay, but again, should we not heat our home?

Or use any electricity? How will we keep our food cold? Cook our food? Heat our water? Charge our phones?"

"The Sampsons have solar panels on their roof. Why can't we get those?"

"If the state ever switches us over to solar panels, then fine, we'll use them," Mom said. "But it's a pretty big commitment to get huge solar panels drilled into our roof. And if we do it, that's two houses on our whole street. I know your heart is in the right place, but a few people here and there installing solar panels won't stop the climate from getting warmer. I just don't think you need to be worrying about this. You're twelve."

"Do you worry about it?" I asked.

"Honestly? Not really. I know I can't fix it. And maybe I just don't know that much about it."

"Mom, you work for a newspaper!"

"Yes, Mia, and my preference is to not read about climate change. There's a guy at work who makes comments about it all the time. It drives us all nuts. He seems angry and bitter. He's always talking like the world is about to end. That's no way to live. Especially when you're a kid."

Mom took a deep breath and sort of offered me an olive branch. "I'll tell you what," she said, probably just trying to get me off her back. "We'll pay closer attention to the electricity we use. We'll really make sure we recycle everything that can be recycled. We'll be more aware of it."

"Will you even make Nate do it?" I asked.

Mom half-smiled. "Yes. I'll make Nate do it. But I'd like you not to get so worked up about it. Okay?"

I nodded, but I didn't mean it. And I'm sure Mom knew that.

Chapter

The Saturday afternoon before school resumed, I spent the day with Rebecca. I was so happy to see my best friend again. We played basketball at the local elementary school courts, though there was more chatting and laughing than shooting the ball.

I told her all about my trip to Chicago, everything from pizza to shopping and more pizza. I also talked about the rally, my new friend Hector, and some of what I had learned from Uncle James about climate change.

"I just don't understand how we're causing so many problems to the climate," I said, "but it's like no one seems to care. I mean, how many times have you heard about climate change in your life?"

Rebecca laughed and rolled her eyes.

I was slightly annoyed, but also somewhat amused by her reaction. I had seen it before. "What?" I demanded.

"Mia, I love you, but you and your causes."

"Becks, this is serious."

"Maybe. It was also serious when you were going to cure homelessness. And racism. And what was the one this summer? Helping the piping plovers at the beach?"

I laughed and playfully tossed the basketball at her.

"Hey!" she jokingly shouted. "It's the truth. Let it set you free!"

The next day, the last before school resumed, we decided as a family to visit Don at the hospital. But when we were heading toward the car, we noticed a pickup truck in Don's driveway. So we walked over.

As we approached the front yard, I spotted a few suitcases in the back of the truck. A man walked out the front door.

"You got here before I got to you," he said to us. "You must be the Dubois family. I'm Ben. Don's my dad."

"Oh, nice to finally meet you, Ben," said Mom.

"I'll say the same to you. I also want to thank you. You guys are my personal heroes." He walked closer to us so we could have a real conversation. "If you hadn't stopped here the night of the storm, I'm not sure what would have happened. You may have saved his life.

"And Mia." He looked down at me, which took me a little by surprise. "Your note—he showed it to every doctor and nurse who came into his room." I was a little embarrassed by the attention, but also glad to have lifted Don's spirits.

"Is he okay?" I asked. That's what we were all dying to hear.

"Yes and no," Ben said. "I mean, he can't walk, and at his age, honestly, I'm not sure if he'll ever walk again. He's eighty-six and has a heart condition. He gets tired easily, and that's with two good legs." Then his face brightened a bit. "But above the waist, he's the same guy. And he's alive. A lot of emotions the last few weeks, but we're mostly relieved. And grateful to you all."

I wasn't sure how to take the news.

"Where is he?" Dad asked.

"He's at a rehab home a little ways from here, closer to Beth. He'll be living there for a while until he heals and regains some of his strength. After that, we'll see."

If Don couldn't get around on his own, how could he live alone? I couldn't help but wonder if he would be moving closer to Beth permanently.

"Please tell him that we miss him, and we wish him a speedy recovery," Mom said.

"I will," Ben said. "Thank you so much."

We agreed that we'd visit him another day soon.

I wished I could shoot baskets at the hoop across the street that afternoon. I loved doing that. And being out there alone, the rhythmic bounce of the ball on the street, the occasional swish as it fell through the net—it was like nothing could bother me (unless my shot was off that day). I could be with my thoughts, distracted by nothing except for occasional passing cars or bikes.

But with the Dwyers' hoop now gone, thanks to Reggie, I sat on our front steps instead, letting my mind wander. I thought about the hoop and the storm that knocked it down. And the tree that thankfully did not crush my family and me.

My mind also drifted to Don. It was weird, but I had rarely thought twice about seeing him wave to me on my way to the bus stop. I always smiled and waved back, but it was more of just a polite thing to do, and a part of my morning routine. Now, though, if he was no longer there to wave to me, I'd really miss it. I'd miss him.

Then I remembered something Uncle James had said in Chicago. Storms like Reggie were becoming more common. I remembered a girl in my class from Puerto Rico who had such a hard time in 2017 when two hurricanes pounded the island in the same month. She apparently had family there and was really stressed about it.

And what about Hector? His life had been forever changed by all sorts of pollution.

Humans were contributing to this destruction.

And almost no one around me seemed to truly care.

I needed to change that.

2

The
Climate
Club

"**D**on't forget your water bottle!" Mom yelled to me as I frantically rushed to get to the bus stop on time.

I was nearly sprinting as I passed her at the front door.

"Have a good day," Mom said. "Love you!"

"Love you too, Mom."

Even though my backpack and I were basically flying down the street to the corner where the bus picked me up, I still took a peak at Don's door. Usually, only the storm door was closed. It had a full glass panel, and Don was almost always sitting in his armchair, which was about six feet inside the door. From that light blue chair, he'd smile and wave.

That day, of course, the main door was also closed. Don wasn't home. I knew he wouldn't be. It still felt like a punch in the gut to see it for real.

I was happy to be back in school. Since I wasn't in Chicago anymore, hanging around at home with Nate and my parents wasn't working for me. And I missed my friends.

Homeroom was pretty awkward that morning, since no one really knew how to act after an unscheduled vacation. Some of us made small talk about the storm and what we did during those two weeks. But once first period rolled around, school was school.

"So that hasn't changed," Rebecca said to me during lunch. We were the first two to sit at our table.

"What hasn't?"

"Matt O'Connor still can't stop staring at you," Rebecca said, despite—or due to—the fact that it annoyed me every time she said it.

"Ugh. You're still on that?" I said disgustedly.

"Come on, Mia. Stop pretending you don't notice it. I bet he's your secret admirer."

"Oh geez," I said. "I forgot all about that thing."

Okay, I may need to backtrack here. See, the day before Reggie, a note had mysteriously appeared in my locker, and I had no clue who had written it. Someone had obviously slid it through the vents on the locker door. The note read:

Hope you like 7th grade so far.

That was it.

Hope you like 7th grade so far.

I did like it so far. What's it to you? Who *are* you?

I had asked my friends about it at lunch that day, but they all denied authorship. One of my close friends, Ariana, pointed out something I had overlooked—or maybe preferred not to acknowledge: "It's clearly a boy's handwriting," she said. Ariana was very intrigued. Among my friends, she had been interested in boys first and, let's say, with the most enthusiasm.

"I think you have a secret admirer or something," she said with a smile.

I grimaced. "No, Ari. Just, no."

"It's not a bad thing."

Yes it was! Not only did boys not interest me, but I saw how much attention "couples" received from their classmates. I *really* didn't want that. The last thing I needed was to have people whispering about me and some boy.

When Reggie happened, and Don, and Chicago, the note had basically fallen out of my brain. So when Rebecca brought it up at lunch the first day back at school, I rolled my eyes.

"What's so bad about having a secret admirer?" she said. "I think it's kind of cool."

"Yeah, I'm not interested."

"In Matt, or boys in general?"

"Well, both. But mostly him. Actually, both."

I knew that Matt O'Connor was a popular kid, and that he was as into basketball as I was. He was also an excellent student, and the other girls seemed to consider him to be pretty cute.

And that was kind of the problem for me. Matt acted too much like he was all of those things. Like he was in love with himself.

He also thought he was hilarious. He'd try to make people laugh in class, and some people would, but he was not funny. I pitied the people who laughed at his lame attempts at humor. Sometimes it actually annoyed me. A shy girl named Liana once rushed into math class late, carrying her trumpet case, when she stepped on one of Matt's binders, lost her balance, and fell on the floor. Instead of helping Liana, or at least having some remorse, he blurted out, "That's gonna leave a mark!" Half the class laughed. I wanted to throw something at all of those heartless jerks. Like, this is what you find funny? Those are your standards for comedy?

Suddenly, Matt took a seat right next to Rebecca at our lunch table. I was completely caught off guard. I tried to pretend I didn't notice him.

"Did you guys have a good break?" he asked. Then, without waiting for an answer, he turned to me. "I heard you went to Chicago."

"Yeah. I visited my uncle." I didn't mean for my tone to come off as rude, but I think it did. I can't say I felt bad about it.

"Nice," he said. Then it seemed like he was waiting for someone to say something that would allow him to stay longer. I had no plans to help him.

"What did you do during the break?" Rebecca finally asked him, probably because it had gotten awkward.

"Sports mostly," he said. "Our football team had a game on Saturday. We won. I scored three touchdowns."

I forced a phony smile, and Rebecca blurted out a half-hearted, "Oh cool." But I think she knew that this bragging was exactly why I found Matt O'Connor so obnoxious. Mercifully, he got up and walked back to his table.

After lunch, Rebecca and I chatted as we strolled to the seventh-grade wing. We stopped at our lockers so that we could switch materials for our afternoon classes. As I squatted down to exchange binders, I noticed a torn piece of loose-leaf paper. It was another note. The handwriting was the same as the first one. It read:

Glad to be able to see you around school again.
You have a nice smile.

A nice smile? Oh no. Maybe I did have a secret admirer! Unless someone was just messing with me, which would be just plain mean. I looked around to see if anyone noticed me reading the note. I hoped no one did, unless it was the author, giving away his identity.

Rebecca met me back at my locker on her way to social studies class.

"Another note?" she asked.

"Yeah."

She quickly read it. "*Nice smile*?" She laughed a sinister laugh. "You *totally* have a secret admirer."

"Shhh!"

"Fine, fine. But seriously, this is so cool. I'm telling you, it's Matt O'Connor."

Again, I rolled my eyes. "I hope not."

We finished chatting just as we entered Mr. Walker's social studies class. I actually liked most of my classes. Science was fun. I did well in math, even if I was by no means excited about it. I liked English, though I didn't always love the books they made us read, so sometimes I would ignore those and read ones that actually interested me.

Social studies, though, had been one of my favorite classes in past years, but this year, the subject matter was ancient history. Neanderthals. Mesopotamia. Sounded boring.

I liked Mr. Walker, though, and on that day, he said something that caught my attention.

"For thousands of years," Mr. Walker said, "the people of the Indian subcontinent have relied on the monsoon rains. It gives them food and water. It gives them life."

I was usually somewhat reluctant to raise my hand in class, but with climate change still very much on my mind, I had a thought. My hand shot up, almost as if beyond my control.

"You have a question, Mia?"

"Yes. Has climate change affected the monsoons? I mean, do they still get the monsoon rains?"

Mr. Walker seemed taken aback. Obviously, my climate change question was totally out of the blue.

He finally responded. "That's a great question, Mia. Actually, yes, it has affected the monsoons. Sometimes they come late now. And when they do come, oftentimes they're extra intense, so they cause more flooding and don't help the crops as much as they once did."

I shook my head in disappointment.

"What made you curious about that, Mia?" Mr. Walker asked.

"It's just frustrating," I said. "That we're causing all these problems."

"We?"

"Yeah. That humans have messed up the climate and all."

"I can see why you'd feel that way." I'd heard adults talk like that before. It must be in the "How To Handle Upset Kids" manual—say something to validate their feelings or something. *Yes, yes, I understand. That would bother me, too.*

Just before the bell to end class, Mr. Walker said something else that stuck with me.

"Tomorrow we'll talk a bit about sub-Saharan Africa. That's Africa south of the Sahara Desert. And then we'll be done with our overview of this year's units, so we can dive right into Early Man on Wednesday."

Africa? We learned in sixth grade that much of Africa was often oppressively hot, and that many people lived without water or enough food. I wondered how climate change was disrupting life there.

Instead of waiting to ask Mr. Walker the next day, I was going to figure it out on my own that night.

Rebecca and I walked toward our last class together, parting ways when I had to turn to art while she continued to health. From there we would get on our separate buses, so we wouldn't see each other until the next day.

"I'll text you later," Rebecca said. "I'm still so glad I can say that to you now!"

"Me too!" I said.

Chapter

I got home from school a few minutes before three o'clock. No one else was there; my parents were working, and Nate was at cross country practice. On my tippy-toes, I reached into the cabinet and grabbed a package of peanut butter crackers. Then I poured some water and sat down at the kitchen table to start my homework.

I generally did my homework as soon as I got home, but today, in particular, I was determined to wrap it up quickly so I could move on to another project.

I started with math. Fifteen minutes and done. Next was science. It was a quick review to help us remember what we were learning before Reggie. Took me ten minutes. I probably rushed through it. Whatever. My English assignment was to read two chapters in our novel. I opted to leave that for later in the evening.

I took a few long, purposeful strides—long by my standards, anyway—into the living room, grabbed the Chromebook, and returned to the kitchen. As soon as I logged in, Google was staring back at me, all but begging to guide me through my search.

"Climate change in Africa." For some reason, I said those words aloud as I typed them in the search bar. I pressed return. The search results page was jaw-dropping.

"Severe consequences for Africa," read the headline from the United Nations website.

"The African continent will be hit hardest by climate change," BBC.com informed me.

I clicked on one article. Then another. I learned that the already oppressive heat in Africa will intensify. Droughts will worsen. Rain patterns will become even less predictable. Rivers will dry up. Africa's amazing wildlife will shrink in numbers, even more than it already had.

I half-wondered if all of this was real, or if I had accidentally keyed in some magic code that unlocked a dark sci-fi portion of the Internet. *How is this possible?*

The next article was upsetting enough that I had to pause for the words to sink in. It explained that most countries in Africa were the least responsible for climate change, since they had burned a fraction of the fossil fuels that countries like the U.S. had. Yet they were among the places being hit the hardest.

I wanted to yell at the computer.

In sixth grade, we had learned about some of the awful things that had happened to Africa over the years: Africans captured and sold as slaves; land conquered and its resources stolen by powerful European countries. So many people there didn't have enough food, couldn't afford school, didn't even have electricity.

And things may only get worse? Because of us? This isn't fair!

I texted Rebecca: "What are you doing?"

She responded: "YouTube. Why?"

I called her.

"Everything okay?" she asked.

"Yes," I said. "Well, not really. You gotta get on your computer and go to Google."

"Okay. What the heck? Is something wrong?"

"Are you there yet?"

"Geez, just a second. Okay, what? Google?"

I think Rebecca expected to see a shocking image on the Google homepage. I told her, "Type in 'climate change in Africa.'"

"Oh, Mia. Really? You're my best friend, and I love you, but you need to chill with—"

"Come on! Just type it in, Becks!"

She sighed. "Fine."

"Okay, do you see what it says?"

"About Africa getting hit the hardest? And severe consequences?"

"Yeah. Click on the third article."

"Mia, it would be a lot easier if you would just tell me what you want me to know."

"Did you click on it yet?"

"Yeah."

"Okay, third paragraph. Read it."

It was silent for about twenty seconds.

"What does that mean?" she asked. "Countries like us and Great Britain have been causing problems for Africa?"

"Yes! We keep using gas in cars, coal and oil for electricity, and so much of it. It's messing up the climate for the whole world. But the poorest countries, the ones that don't do that stuff as much, are gonna suffer. They already are."

Rebecca was silent.

"Becks?" I said.

"Did you read the whole thing?" Rebecca asked.

"Yeah. It's awful."

"You see a few paragraphs down where 'effects of climate change' is underlined? I wonder what that's about."

We both clicked on it. It brought us to an article with a headline that read: "New study reveals dire climate forecast." We each read it silently.

It said that the global temperature had already risen about one degree Celsius—just as I had learned in Chicago. It also said that each small increase in the temperature would cause big problems for the climate.

And that a few years ago, countries around the world had vowed to limit global warming to two, or even one and a half degrees Celsius, but that almost no progress had been made to slow down emissions. That felt like the cherry on top of the melting sundae.

We read that if nothing was done, no real changes made, the temperature, by 2100, could rise five degrees Celsius, according to some estimates.

"How much is that Fahrenheit?" I wondered aloud.

"I'll check," Rebecca said. She Googled something. "Wait, that can't be. Hang on. It looks like nine degrees Fahrenheit."

I couldn't believe it. "Nine?" I shouted. "Are you sure? The average temperature might be nine degrees hotter in 2100? We could still be alive in 2100!"

"This other article says Miami could be gone by then," Rebecca reported. "Like, underwater. Crap. I always wanted to go there."

I was heated. "And *we* are doing this!"

"Dude," Rebecca said. "We kinda suck."

We were momentarily silent. Processing.

"Why are we not hearing more about this?" Rebecca said. "From our parents? In school?"

"This is what I'm saying, Becks. When my Uncle James told me a little of this, I couldn't believe it. My mom said some stuff about not wanting me to worry. But, I mean, somebody has to worry. Right?"

"Seriously. What the heck, Mia? How am I supposed to concentrate on other stuff now? I need my parents to get home so I can yell at them!"

"I did that the other day. Didn't go well."

That night, I struggled, too, to concentrate on my reading assignment. So I read more about climate change, using my phone because Nate needed the Chromebook for his homework.

My phone buzzed at about eight o'clock. It was a text from Rebecca.

"What can we do about this climate change thing?" the text read.

"IDK," I responded. "Something. Definitely something."

Chapter

The next day, I had social studies class during first period, and after what I had read the night before, I couldn't wait to start a discussion about climate change. But before that, I decided to talk to my homeroom teacher, Mrs. Young, who was also my science teacher. I figured that if any of my teachers would know about climate change, it would be Mrs. Young.

I didn't know her very well. She had missed the first couple of weeks of the school year on maternity leave after having her first baby. In fact, her first week was the week before Reggie. So I had spent about six days in class with her.

As other kids gradually filed into homeroom that morning, I approached Mrs. Young's desk.

"Mrs. Young?"

"Hi, Mia. How's it going this morning?"

"Okay. How are you?"

"All right. Good, actually, because I'm still trying really hard to learn everyone's name, and I just got yours right." She smiled. "So, what's up?"

"I wanted to ask you, do we learn about climate change in seventh grade?"

"Mmm, not really," she said. "It comes up a little. You'll learn more about it in eighth grade, and then some in high school."

"It's really bad, right?"

"Climate change?"

"Yeah."

"Well, it's not good," she said.

"Shouldn't we be learning about it?"

"You didn't learn about it at all in elementary school?"

"Barely. That we need to respect the planet and recycle and stuff. That's basically it."

Mrs. Young sighed. "It's tough, Mia. We have a certain curriculum we need to cover."

"But what's more important than that?" I asked. "The Earth's temperature rising and people suffering? That seems more important than anything else we would learn."

"I don't disagree with you, Mia. It sounds like you know a bit about it. I think a lot of people believe we shouldn't worry kids by focusing on it too much right now."

I grimaced. "But is anyone focusing on it? Is anything actually being done?"

"Yes, for sure. There are groups that raise awareness, protest, try to change laws. Especially young adults. And more energy is coming from solar and wind now."

"But I read that the United States actually gets worse almost every year. More greenhouse gases or something."

Mrs. Young paused, then said, "We should talk more about this another time. The bell's about to ring, and I need to take attendance. But we should definitely discuss it more."

"Okay," I said. "Thanks." At least she didn't tell me to just forget about it. I took my seat for the morning announcements. I listened to none of them.

After the bell rang, I saw Rebecca on the way into social studies class.

"Hey Becks."

"Hey Mia. You gonna ask him about that Africa stuff?"

"Yeah."

A few minutes into class, I saw my opening. Mr. Walker mentioned that humans originated in Africa and that the continent had such diverse wildlife, from giraffes to lions to chimpanzees.

"Yes, Mia?" the teacher said when I raised my hand, somewhat out of the blue since he hadn't asked a question or anything.

"I read yesterday that climate change is hurting Africa more than other continents," I said.

"That's definitely true. No doubt."

"Should our country be doing anything about that? To help them?"

"It's *Africa*," snarked a boy named Braden. "And what's with you and climate change all of a sudden?"

"Shut up, Braden!" Rebecca said, looking directly at him. I love her.

Braden started to respond to Rebecca when Mr. Walker entered the fray. "Both of you, stop," he said firmly. "Mia was the one with her hand up. Mia, would you like to explain what you mean?"

I now felt somewhat embarrassed and uncomfortable by the whole thing. The last thing I expected was for a kid to criticize me for asking a question that I considered important. That everyone should consider important. I almost shook my head no, but I pressed on and forced myself to talk.

"Well, this article that Rebecca and I saw said that we cause more damage to the climate than basically any other country. Countries in Africa don't do as much. But climate change is worse for them than us. I guess that just seems unfair."

"I love that you're interested in this," Mr. Walker said. "And you're right. We're doing very little. You know what? I'd like to talk to you about it after class."

I nodded, hoping he would follow through on that and not just hope I'd forget to bring it up again. When class ended, I walked toward Mr. Walker. Rebecca followed.

"You wanted to talk to me?" I said.

"Yes, Mia. Why don't you come have lunch with me today? Climate change is a really important topic, and I'd be very interested to discuss it with you. I just want to keep the class focused on the day's lesson so we don't fall behind."

"Okay."

"Can I come too?" Rebecca asked. "I physically can't eat without Mia. My stomach would reject the food. And that would get messy."

I don't think Mr. Walker was totally sure how to react to Rebecca's humor. He was still getting to know us, after all.

"Sure," he said. "You're not going to tell anyone to shut up, are you?"

"Only Mia." We all laughed. Even Mr. Walker.

"Okay then. See you both at lunch."

"You think it'll be weird?" I asked Rebecca as we walked with our lunch bags to Mr. Walker's classroom.

"I don't think so. He seems pretty cool. I mean, he didn't get mad at my weird jokes."

"Yeah. And they *were* weird. You basically said you'd throw up if you didn't eat with me."

"Did I go too far?"

"I don't know. I thought it was funny."

As we entered the room, Mr. Walker was drizzling French dressing on his salad, and he looked up from his desk chair. "Have a seat, girls. Glad you came."

After a little small talk about Reggie, Mr. Walker asked me about my recent interest in climate change.

"I visited my uncle in Chicago last week," I said. "He told me a lot about it. And he took me to a climate rally downtown."

"Oh, interesting. I was born in Chicago. South Side. Went to the University of Chicago."

"Really? I love it there. In Chicago, I mean."

"Where does your uncle live?"

"On the North Side. I think it's called Ravenswood."

"Yeah, Ravenswood. Same city, but it's like a different world from where I grew up."

Mr. Walker was one of only two Black teachers at the middle school. I remembered a couple of the Black speakers at the rally talking about the South Side. Then I thought about Hector and his neighborhood in East City.

"How did you end up in Plymouth?" asked Rebecca.

88   Chris Casavant

"I met a girl in college who is from the Boston area. After college, I moved to Boston to be close to her. Then I decided to become a teacher, so I went to grad school and did my student teaching here."

"Are you glad you came out here?" Rebecca asked.

He chuckled. "Well yeah, I married the girl. I do miss my family back in Chicago, but I like it here. Not as many people look like me here, though."

It was interesting to learn about Mr. Walker outside of school. To that point, he had mainly just spoken about maps and studying ancient civilizations. Maybe I was listening too much, though, because as Mr. Walker took occasional bites of his salad, I realized I had not touched my turkey sandwich.

"So Mia," he said, "you mentioned that you went to a rally?"

"Yeah. And I met a kid from East City who has health problems because of the pollution there."

"East City. They've had some major issues there. I knew a kid in college from there. We still keep in touch a little."

I continued on. "And then yesterday, me and Rebecca were reading these articles about climate change and how bad it is. And how much worse it'll get. Like when we're old, the planet could be five degrees Celsius warmer."

"Nine degrees Fahrenheit!" Rebecca blurted out.

"Well," Mr. Walker said, "I have good news and bad news. Things have improved a bit in the last few years, so we're now headed for more like three degrees Celsius, not five. The bad news is, that's still way too much."

I wasn't sure if that was comforting or not.

"Hardly anyone talks to us about it," I continued. "Not our parents. Teachers either. Not really, anyway."

"I tried talking to my parents about it last night," Rebecca said. "They think climate change is when it rains one day and is sunny the next. They were clueless. For real."

Mr. Walker and I laughed.

"I'm gonna be very honest with you both," Mr. Walker said. "When I was in college, like ten to twelve years ago now, I went to some rallies and protests about climate change. I even wrote something for the school newspaper about it, that we should be more focused on it. And especially cleaning up the pollution in some of the poor neighborhoods in and around Chicago. But I got so frustrated that nothing was getting done. Fossil fuel companies have so much money that it seemed impossible to ever beat them."

He shook his head. "So I basically gave up. I felt like I was playing a basketball game where I was the only one on my team, but the other team had five LeBron Jameses. And in five years here, few students have really mentioned it much. But it is very important, and I'm happy to keep talking with you about it throughout the year."

I was about to accept that invitation when an idea was suddenly launched from Rebecca's mouth. "Maybe we should start a club! You know, like drama or newspaper or whatever. The Climate Club!"

I looked at her and smiled. A club? I hadn't thought about a club, but I sort of loved the idea.

Mr. Walker gently nodded his head. "Climate Club. Interesting. What if you're the only two kids in it?"

"Well, when Mia's focused on something, she's worth at least five kids," Rebecca joked.

Mr. Walker chuckled. "I would be curious to see

if other students are interested in it. I'll need to talk it over with Principal Lewis, and then figure out what day works best for me. I'll get back to you girls. Now Mia, eat that sandwich. The bell's about to ring."

I scarfed down the sandwich, but I can't say I savored it. My mind was already focused on the Climate Club, even if it wasn't an official thing yet.

Chapter

I texted Rebecca that night.

"You're a genius."

"I know." A minute passed before she sent me a follow-up: "What did I do?"

"The Climate Club idea!"

"Oh right. That was pretty genius. Let me guess, you're making plans already."

I texted back a winking emoji.

In fact, there were so many ideas that I feared some would escape my brain. Since plugging my ears and nose wouldn't work, I jotted down as many as I could capture.

Most importantly, I wanted other students and teachers to start caring about the environment as much as I did. Now that I knew what I knew, I was certain that others would quickly rally behind the cause.

After all, the world was changing, and not for the better. Humans were making it worse. *How could anyone not care about that?*

The next morning, I left the house early, eager to get to school. I had time to walk into Don's front yard. Only his old car occupied space in the driveway. The front door was still closed.

I sat on his front steps and opened my backpack. I grabbed a notebook and pen and scratched out a quick note:

Mr. Francis,
We're all thinking about you and hoping you
are feeling better. It's weird not seeing you on
my way to the bus stop. Hope to see you soon.
Love,
Mia

I had wanted to write another note, especially after hearing how much he appreciated my other one. I carefully tore out the page from my notebook, folded it in half, and placed it between the storm and main doors, closing the storm door to ensure it was safe. Then I walked to the bus stop.

When I arrived at school, I quickly gathered the materials I'd need for first period, shoved the rest of my stuff into my locker, and gave it a kick for good measure so I could completely close the door.

But as I peered over my shoulder, I noticed a piece of paper sticking out of the locker. I grabbed it. It was another note. Same handwriting as the previous two. And it was just as concise:

Good luck on your math quiz today.

Math quiz? The seventh grade had three teams, each with eighty or so kids. So at first, I assumed the notes must be coming from a boy on my team. But then

I remembered that the day before, my friend Ariana, who is on a different team, mentioned having to study for a math quiz. I had no clue who this could be.

I shoved the note in my bag and weaved through the crowded morning hallway, passed by my homeroom, and darted into Mr. Walker's class.

"Hey Mia!" called a voice.

I briefly stopped and looked around. It was Matt O'Connor. I forced a half-smile and then continued on my mission to talk to Mr. Walker.

I waited for him to finish chatting with a student. When it was my turn, I got right to the point. "Did you talk to Principal Lewis yet?"

Mr. Walker looked befuddled. "Huh?"

"About the Climate Club?"

"Oh! Yes, I actually did. She loves the idea. And it looks like Wednesdays work the best for me. Is that okay with you?"

"I think so. I'll make it work anyway."

"Perfect! I'll put something in the announcements. Rebecca is still in, right?"

"Yes," I confirmed. "She has no choice anyway. I'll make her do it."

Mr. Walker laughed, and I turned to walk out of the room. I made sure not to make eye contact with Matt O'Connor, who was talking loudly to his friends, like he was trying to get my attention. Typical. As I reached the doorway, I heard Mr. Walker tell Matt to quiet down, which made me smile for real. I didn't have to force it.

But that wasn't my last encounter with Matt O'Connor that day. There was one more, and it showed me what I, and the Climate Club, might be up against.

Toward the end of lunch, I walked from my table toward the trash to throw out my empty granola bar wrapper. As I approached within a few feet of the barrel, an empty plastic water bottle, tossed from some distance away, flew into the barrel, clanging against the inside before settling amongst the trash.

"O'Connor for three!" I heard. As I turned around, there was Matt O'Connor, looking at me with a big smile and both of his arms raised, like a basketball referee signaling a three-pointer.

I scowled. "There's a recycle bin for those," I said, making no attempt to conceal my disdain.

"Who cares?" he said.

I do!

I abruptly turned and walked back to my seat. I guess it didn't bode well for my cause that one of the most popular kids in seventh grade thought recycling was a joke.

Recycling. That was the most basic way to address environmental problems. Everyone learned in elementary school that plastic bottles basically never decompose, and that many of them find their way into bodies of water, causing all kinds of problems for sea life. How could the Climate Club accomplish anything if kids didn't even take *recycling* seriously?

When I returned to my seat, I angrily recounted the story for my friends. I normally ate with Rebecca and two of my other close friends, Aliya and Ariana, both of whom had already expressed interest in joining the Climate Club, though Ariana seemed less committed. At least Aliya and Rebecca shared in my outrage at Matt O'Connor.

Then Rebecca stood up.

"Becks, what are you doing?" I asked nervously.

Rebecca didn't answer. Instead, she walked over to the trash. She spotted the water bottle, reached in, and pulled it out. She scanned the area and found Matt O'Connor's table.

"Hey Matt!" she yelled. He looked up at her. She held the bottle over the adjacent barrel meant for recyclable plastics. She dropped the bottle in the correct barrel and, still staring at Matt, said, "These go in here. See the big 'Recycle' sign? That's where recycle goes. IN THE RE-CY-CLE BIN."

"Oh my God, you guys are freaks," Matt said, looking at Rebecca and then turning to his friends so that, obviously, he could mock us for making such a big deal about the whole thing.

I was embarrassed. "I can't believe you did that," I said to Rebecca, who had just returned to the table. But I wasn't upset with her. Matt deserved it, and Rebecca was just the person to deliver it.

"That might be the end of your secret admirer notes," Aliya said, laughing.

"Oh yeah, hadn't really thought about that," Rebecca said.

My face brightened as I considered the potential and unexpected side benefit to my friend's actions. "We can only hope."

"I don't know," said Ariana. "I wish he had a crush on me. He's pretty cute."

I made a face like I was gagging on a spoonful of peas.

Chapter

As I approached our driveway after getting off the bus that afternoon, I heard footsteps a little ways behind me. I casually turned around and saw Beth, Don's daughter, briskly walking toward me.

"Mia!"

"Oh, hi!"

Beth took a moment to catch her breath.

"How's it going?" she asked me.

"Good. How's your dad?"

"He's doing okay. He isn't loving being away from home and being surrounded by strangers. But I think that's good, because it'll motivate him to get better."

"Will he come back here?" I asked, referring to his house.

"We don't know what's going to happen yet. We'll have to see what's best for him when he's recovered."

Beth held up a piece of paper and a key on a key ring. I noticed the paper was the note I had written for Don that morning.

"I read your note. It made me a little teary."

I smiled and could feel my face turn reddish. I

was writing the notes to make him happy, but not to be praised.

"It might seem like a simple thing to you," she said, "but this is gonna make him so happy. And my hope is that things like this will push him through his rehab. I know he wants to come back home. He's lived here for forty-two years. We don't know if it can work yet, but reminders of home will only make him more determined to get back here."

"Well, I'm happy to keep writing some notes."

"That'd be great. But I'm here to ask another favor."

"Okay."

"I've been coming down here every few days to pick up his mail. But I live an hour away and I have a lot of other things going on. Last time I was here, his mailbox was completely stuffed, and some things got ruined. I thought if you could get his mail every day, or even every other day, that would be a huge help to us."

"Of course! I'll definitely do that."

Beth exhaled and smiled. "Thank you so much." She seemed relieved, but that was the least I could do.

She handed me the key. "This will get you in the kitchen door. I'll put a cardboard box on the kitchen table. If you can just put the mail in there, I'll pick it up on the weekends."

I opened my backpack and secured the key ring to a clip inside the front pouch. "No problem!"

"Thank you again." Beth glanced at her phone. "I need to get going. I'm gonna stop and see my daughter in Bridgewater. She's having her first baby soon! I'm gonna be a grandma!"

I smiled. Then, as Beth had begun to walk away, she turned around again.

"You should hear him at the rehab center," she said. "He tells everyone over there about the girl he waves to every morning. Tells the same story every time. How he was waving to you when you were so small that your backpack was as big as you. And that now you're so grown up. He shows them the note you wrote him in the hospital."

Then she held up my note from that morning and chuckled.

"I bet this one makes the rounds, too."

"What's new at school?" Mom asked us at dinner that night.

"Nuthin," Nate said. "Math quiz Friday. Cross country meet tomorrow against Marshfield. We're gonna get crushed."

"That's the positive attitude we've worked so hard to instill in our children," Mom cracked. "What about you, Mia?"

"Well, me and Rebecca are starting a club about climate change. Our social studies teacher is gonna run it. Pretty excited about it."

"That's great, Mia. I know that's been on your mind lately. I'm glad you'll have a way to channel that energy of yours."

"What's that club gonna do?" Nate asked. "Are you gonna just go around and yell at people who don't recycle?"

"Nate!" Mom snapped. "Be supportive."

"Well, she's only gonna make people angry. She got so mad at me once because I put a plastic bottle in the trash."

I noticed Mom's furrowed brow and was glad it was directed at Nate. "Well, why would you do that?"

" 'Cause I knew it would tick her off."

"This is why climate change is getting so bad," I said, looking at my food. "Too many idiots."

"Whatever," Nate said.

Then Dad, who had been working in the living room, entered the kitchen at the end of the conversation, finding the whole thing amusing.

"Aren't you glad you asked about their day, honey?" he grinned. Neither Nate nor I flinched.

I spent that night in my room researching climate change on my phone. I read something that Uncle James had told me, which made me think of him. So I took a break and sent him a text.

"I miss you, Uncle James. Thinking about you. We're starting a climate change club at school."

I returned to reading, but a minute or so later, the phone buzzed in my hand.

"One of the many things I love about you," Uncle James had replied. "I knew you'd do something about it. We need you in this fight."

"I'm in it!" I typed back. He sent back a thumbs-up emoji.

I was definitely in it. I just hoped other kids at school could be convinced to jump in, too.

Chapter

Not every morning was the same in our house. Nate typically got a ride to school from one of his friends, who would arrive around 7:10. My bus consistently showed up between 7:33 and 7:36, so I wanted to be out the door at 7:28—it took two minutes to get to the bus stop.

It was not unusual for Dad to be gone before me. He took his job very seriously, perhaps too much so, I thought. How could he be so dedicated to selling washers and dryers that he would miss family dinners or other things that many dads would attend? *He's not saving lives.*

Mom normally left the house last, unless she had a story to cover early in the morning. On this particular morning at 7:15, only Mom and I were still home.

"Don't let your brother get to you," she said as we finished cleaning up after breakfast.

"Please," I said. "I couldn't care less what he says."

"You know...." Mom paused, seeming to gather her thoughts. I felt a lecture coming and was glad I had to be out the door in just a few minutes. Saved by the bus, so to speak.

"He's not a bad kid," Mom continued. "You could stand to be nicer to him."

"*Me* be nicer?" I asked incredulously. "He admitted last night that he hurts the planet to get on my nerves."

"Yeah. Not his finest moment." Mom smiled warmly. "But he does care about you. He's just really laid back about things. And you can be pretty feisty. Maybe you could tone that down sometimes. Don't immediately frown the second he walks in the room either. Ya know?"

"I guess."

"Anyway, this came in the mail for you yesterday." She handed me an envelope. It seemed to be a letter. The outside was written in a kid's handwriting, and the return address was East City. "Do you know who it's from?"

"It must be Hector! The kid I met at the rally in Chicago." My face brightened. "Uncle James must have given him our address."

"Well, that's pretty cool. Bring it with you. You can read it on the bus."

I took my usual seat on the bus, about halfway down the aisle, next to Aliya. Aliya was probably my second-best friend. She was smart and caring, and easily the most reserved in our group of friends. As far as we all knew, she was the only Muslim in the entire school, and until that spring, no one outside of our immediate circle of friends—Ariana, Rebecca, and me—knew that about her.

Then one day, things changed.

It was toward the end of a mid-May day in sixth grade, and Aliya and I were part of a basketball game in gym class. Aliya doesn't enjoy basketball and rarely plays, but she was on my team, and she knew I wanted to win. Being a good friend—and perhaps not wanting to deal with me if we lost—Aliya gave it her all.

After the game ended, she sat down and began to feel light-headed. She leaned forward and I tried to comfort her. The gym teacher, Mrs. Murray, asked which water bottle was Aliya's, but Aliya had no water bottle that day. She couldn't have water, or any food. It was during Ramadan.

When Mrs. Murray told another student to grab a paper cup from her office and fill it up at the bubbler, Aliya said she was fine. Mrs. Murray insisted. That's when Aliya quietly said, "It's Ramadan. I'm Muslim. I can't have anything until tonight."

Unfortunately for her secret, Mrs. Murray wasn't the only one who heard her. And while just about everyone continued to outwardly treat her as they had before that afternoon, some kids would ask her questions. Questions about Islam. She was shy and didn't love the attention. She said she felt like an exhibit at a museum.

Then there was one day over the summer when the four of us were hanging out at the beach. Ariana's mom had driven us, along with Ariana's little sister, and she allowed us to set up a blanket about fifty yards away—far enough so we could have some privacy, but close enough that she could still see us.

There had been a news report the night before of a suicide bomb that killed some U.S. soldiers in the Middle East. This would not ordinarily have even registered with Aliya. First of all, she was born in Boston and had lived in Plymouth since she was two. Second, she said her parents had repeatedly told her that a real Muslim was loving and accepting of others, and thus, would not commit an act of violence against innocent people. And third, until recently, only her closest friends had even known she was Muslim.

As we sat on my big Celtics blanket that day, chatting and laughing, three boys, all recent graduates of the middle school, walked by. Aliya happened to glance up and make eye contact with one of them.

"What are *you* looking at?" the boy said. "Why don't you go back to Eye-rack, or wherever you're from."

We were all stunned. Rebecca glared at them and said, "Why don't you go to hell, or wherever you're from!"

When I looked to my right at Aliya, she just stared into the sand, and a few tears fell from her eyes. I put my arm around her while silently stewing. As Ariana and Rebecca gathered over to comfort Aliya, it occurred to me that no one around us had condemned the boys or shown any concern for my friend. I guess I had always assumed people were better than that.

Since then, I had found myself increasingly drawn to Aliya. We had been friends since second grade when she moved a few streets away from me, but now we were becoming closer than ever.

As I sat down on the bus, I pulled out the letter and showed Aliya. "Look at this!"

"What is it?"

"Remember that kid I told you about that I met in Chicago? The one who has asthma and really cares about the environment?"

"Yeah."

"Well, he sent me a letter. My mom just gave it to me. Haven't even opened it yet."

"Wow, you have a pen pal from Chicago? I'm jealous!"

"Please, you write to your cousins in Yemen!"

"But that's family. This is some kid you met in Chicago."

I opened the letter, and we silently read it together. Hector told me that Uncle James gave him my address and suggested we write to each other. He mentioned that he was writing a book of short stories, but that it was taking him a long time. He'd send me one when he finished. He wondered how I was doing. Almost in passing, he included, "I think we're going to another protest soon. My mom mentioned it. Something about oil. I'll probably see your uncle there."

"Oil?" I wondered aloud.

"Are you gonna write back?" Aliya asked.

"Yeah, for sure."

"So jealous."

"Um, Yemen!"

Aliya smiled and shook her head.

"Finally," Principal Lewis said near the end of that morning's announcements, "we have a new club to tell you about. The Climate Club will educate about the important issue of climate change. Join Mr. Walker in Room 133 next Wednesday after school for the Climate Club's first meeting. If you're interested but can't make it, please let Mr. Walker know. Have a great day, everyone!"

Just what I wanted to hear! I couldn't wait to get started. I wasn't sure how many other students would join, other than Rebecca, Aliya, and Ariana—Ariana hadn't fully committed yet, but I knew I could wear her down.

Later that day, I did learn of someone else who would participate. Science class was ending, and I was about to head to lunch when Mrs. Young called me over to her desk.

"I've thought a lot about what you said to me last week," she said. "About climate change. And Mr. Walker told me about the club you guys are starting. I'm gonna help him with it. I'll be there on Wednesday. This is a really personal issue for me."

"Personal? What do you mean?"

"I'll just leave it at that for now, but I want to be involved. And I'm really glad you're doing this."

"Thanks," I said. "Me too!"

When I walked out of the room, Rebecca, Aliya, and Ariana were waiting to walk with me to lunch.

"What was that about?" Rebecca asked.

"Mrs. Young is gonna help with the Climate Club. She said it's a personal issue for her."

"Personal? What does that mean?"

"I don't know. She wouldn't say." I then turned to Ariana. "You're in, right Ari?"

"I'm thinking about it."

"No, you're in," Rebecca said. "Not a choice. I already signed you up. And I know there's no signup sheet. But in my head, you're signed up."

"I don't know. I've got stuff to do," Ariana annoyingly insisted.

"Come on!" I said. "Softball isn't till the spring. You never practice your violin, and you're amazing at it. You spend five minutes on your homework and get all A's. If anyone doesn't have stuff to do, it's you."

"Will there be any boys there?" Ariana asked. Aliya and Rebecca laughed, while I shook my head in mock disgust.

"Boys are a waste of time," I said. "Trust me. I live with one."

Aliya chimed in. "It'll be fun. Just say yes so we can stop harassing you."

Ariana finally caved. "Okay, fine." She shook her head. "You guys are relentless."

∽

I saw the mail truck driving up my street before I got off the bus that afternoon. It reminded me that I was supposed to start picking up Don's mail.

I reached the bottom of his driveway and opened my backpack to fish out the key. I grabbed the mail from his mailbox, headed for the kitchen door, turned the key, and I was in his kitchen. His house had a distinct odor—neither good nor bad, but distinct nonetheless. It had smelled that way every time I had ever been there. I couldn't help but wonder: do visitors think my house has a smell?

As I placed the mail in the cardboard box on the kitchen table, I noticed some photos nearby. One was of an infant and a toddler. I assumed those were his great-grandchildren in Georgia. Then my attention veered up toward the wall. More photos, these of four adults, younger than my parents. Don's grandchildren?

At that moment, it occurred to me that I had never truly looked around his house, which was weird since he had lived next door to me my whole life. And I had been in there before, to deliver baked goods or drop off a kindness rock that I had painted. Don would take them from me, all smiles as he would ask me questions or crack a couple of jokes. "Fill the container back up and return to me," he'd crack as he gave me back some empty Tupperware from my previous delivery. Nervous about how to have a conversation with someone more than seventy years older than me, I would smile, awkwardly, while fidgeting with the bottom of my shirt, probably making it appear that I couldn't wait to leave. Thinking about this made me feel bad.

I put my backpack down on the kitchen floor and wandered into the living room, where I noticed several old pictures on the wall. They looked like Don as a young man—some with his late wife, others with his children.

Then I spotted one of him in a military uniform, sitting beside the hospital bed of another soldier. Adjacent to that was a photo of Don, again in uniform, saluting. He looked so proud. And handsome!

But the most interesting, by far, was a very small, yellowed, three-paragraph newspaper article with the headline: "Three local men arrested in civil rights protest." The article explained that many had turned out to protest segregation in Boston schools, and Don was one of the three from Plymouth County to be arrested. He felt enough pride in it to hang the article on his living room wall.

That night, I asked Dad about Don. Dad knew him better than anyone else in our house. He would periodically stop by Don's house to check on him, help him with some small repairs around his house, or just chat.

First I asked him about the pictures of Don in military gear.

"Yeah, Don fought in the Korean War," he said. "He's told me a lot about that. He was drafted, and when he went through the physical, he was sore from playing football the day before. He told me they thought he was faking to try to avoid the war!"

"What about the picture of him next to the other soldier's bed?" I asked.

"He helped to save that guy's life! Apparently, the guy had been hit in the leg by a piece of shrapnel and couldn't walk. Don and another soldier got him to safety. He once showed me the medal he got for that. Distinguished service medal, I think."

"Wow!"

"I know. Pretty amazing."

"And the newspaper article about him getting arrested?"

Dad laughed. "He's told me that story so many times, I feel like I was there. He had two small children at home, and when his wife found out he had been arrested, she was furious. She bailed him out of jail but didn't talk to him for a week!"

"So he supported civil rights?"

"Yeah, at a time when not many white people were willing to protest like that. It's pretty impressive."

"Did he know Martin Luther King or Rosa Parks?" These were the two famous civil rights figures I knew the most about from elementary school.

"Oh, goodness no. He just protested a couple of times. But it was pretty gutsy. Don is a fascinating guy. You should talk to him sometime. The guy can tell quite a story."

I actually *really* wanted to do that, especially now that I knew more about his past. I hoped he would move back home so I'd get that chance. I wanted to ask him all about his life, which was apparently far more interesting than I ever imagined.

Chapter

"All right!" an enthusiastic Mr. Walker said. "This is a pretty good turnout!"

Mrs. Young agreed. "Yeah. More than I expected."

I was one of twenty-four students who attended the first Climate Club meeting. They included students from the sixth, seventh, and eighth grades, though half of them came from our seventh-grade team.

I felt a little anxious about the first meeting. Since Rebecca and I were really the ones who started all the talk about climate change in Mr. Walker's class, I wanted so much for it to succeed and make a difference. But if the other kids didn't like it, or felt like it was a waste of time, the whole thing could flop.

Mr. Walker and Mrs. Young introduced themselves and congratulated all of us on choosing to do something positive with our free time. They asked us to introduce ourselves and explain why we had decided to attend this first meeting.

The most common answers dealt with recycling

and littering. "It bothers me so much to see trash on the ground," one student said.

"I skate down at the park, and a lot of times, we have to pick up wrappers and plastic cups just to use the ramp," added another. "It's so annoying."

But one student's answer really stood out. To me, at least.

"Hi, my name's Christian Pereira," he began. Christian was a seventh-grader on Ariana's team, the "blue" team, whereas Rebecca, Aliya, and I were on the "red" team.

"I chose to join the Climate Club because I'm so frustrated that the world is not making enough changes, even though we know things are getting worse," he continued. "My grandparents were from Brazil, and I have cousins who live there. The Amazon rainforest is getting burned, and it's killing animals and making the planet hotter. And it's mostly so people can have more beef. I just can't believe we're allowing all this to happen."

I had seen Christian before, but to be honest, until then, I hadn't even known his name—we'd attended different elementary schools and were not in the same sixth or seventh grade classes. But now, I found myself interested in every word he had to say. He seemed as bothered by climate change as I was.

Then Mr. Walker pointed to Mrs. Young, who was nodding.

"This is a big deal, what's happening in the Amazon, and it's rarely talked about around here," Mrs. Young said. "When you all think of climate change and its causes, what comes to mind?"

Hands went up. Cars. Planes. Heat. Littering. Plastic.

"All big problems," Mrs. Young said. "But the meat, and especially beef, is as bad as any of them."

"This is why Mrs. Young is a vegan," Mr. Walker said. "I've cut down on meat since college, but she is really committed to it."

Wait, beef was a problem? *Beef?* I was surprised and a bit confused, and when I glanced around the room, I noticed that others seemed to feel the same way.

"How is beef making the planet warmer?" asked Ariana, whose interest was suddenly piqued.

Mrs. Young looked at Christian. "Do you know?"

"I think so," he said. "Forests take in a lot of carbon dioxide, which helps with pollution. And they're burning down forests to make room for cows to graze. It's so stupid."

Mrs. Young nodded and then elaborated. "When trees get burned, there's a few problems. First of all, they release all the carbon they have stored over all those years. And second, they're no longer there to hold more carbon in the future."

This was a new side of Mrs. Young. To me, she had seemed flustered at times since returning to school from maternity leave, like she was trying to play catch-up all the time. She would apologize for little mistakes, like mixing up her science terms or opening the wrong document on her computer, and when that happened, it would often come with a mention of how tired she was, that her baby was keeping her awake. I felt bad for her. But now, she seemed totally in her comfort zone.

"In a place like the Amazon," she continued, "all of the trees create humidity, which leads to rain. The rainforest basically makes its own weather. Less trees, less rain. Less rain, less plants and animals survive there."

I had spent a fair amount of time on the Internet researching climate change, but this was news to me. Like most families I knew, we had burgers, steak, pot roast—we even ate all-beef hot dogs because Mom said they were healthier. Healthier for who, I now wondered?

"That's not the end of the problems with the meat industry," Mr. Walker added. "As you can imagine, cows eat. A lot. They're huge animals. And a lot of the cows that get turned into beef that's sold in stores, they eat corn. So we're growing and transporting all this corn, and while people are starving around the world, this corn is being fed to cows to fatten them up so we can eat them."

Some of the other kids in the room exchanged promises about never eating beef again. But I was too distracted. Again, how did I not know this? That very day, beef tacos had been virtually inhaled by hundreds of kids in the school cafeteria. If beef was so bad for the planet, why did it seem to be everywhere?

"At our next meeting," Mr. Walker said as the meeting came to a close, "we'll start to talk about some action plans. Things we can do to make a difference. This was a great meeting."

Mrs. Young agreed. "Absolutely. Great job, everyone. I'm inspired by you guys right now!"

My friends clustered together as everyone gathered their bags and coats. Some texted parents to check on their rides. Others began walking to pick up the late bus. But I made a beeline toward Christian.

"That was really interesting about the Amazon," I said. "I had no idea."

"Yeah. It's crazy."

"Do your cousins live anywhere near the rainforest?"

"Not really. But they want to protect it. They care about it."

About ten seconds of awkward silence followed before Christian thankfully broke it. "I heard you started this club."

"Well, sort of. I mean, I talked to Mr. Walker about climate change because it bothers me so much. My friend had the idea for the club."

"I was happy to hear about it. I talk to my parents about it all the time. They're sick of hearing about it."

"Yeah, I understand. Believe me."

Christian continued. "I have a little sister. She's nine. I explain this stuff to her a lot, and she actually listens. She once got in trouble at school for telling a kid he needs to stop eating a hamburger. The teacher thought she was calling the kid fat."

We both cracked up. Especially me.

"I have a brother in high school," I said. "He's an idiot. He throws plastic bottles in the trash just to make me angry. What he doesn't realize is that I was already angry from looking at his face."

Christian thought that was pretty funny.

"I gotta go so I don't miss the late bus," he said. "You taking the bus?"

"No. My friend's mom is picking us up."

"Okay. Well, see ya later."

"Yeah, see ya."

As Christian left, I turned around to see my friends all staring at me with grins on their faces.

"Wait," Ariana said. "Somebody recently said that boys were a waste of time. Becks, who was that again?"

"I don't remember. Aliya, was it you?"

"No, I don't think so," Aliya said. "But I do remember someone saying that. If I could only remember who it was."

"You guys are crazy," I said. "You didn't find it interesting, what he said?"

"Not as interesting as you did, apparently," said Ariana, who was enjoying the whole thing a little too much.

I just shook my head and grabbed my backpack, hoping their teasing was over but fearing it wasn't. As if this whole secret admirer thing wasn't bringing enough unwanted attention. We walked toward the front door of the school and then outside, where we spotted Aliya's mom's car.

"I can't wait to tell Aliya's mom that Mia has a boyfriend now," Rebecca said.

I could feel my face turning red. "Becks, I'll never speak to you again. Seriously!"

"Fine, fine." Rebecca could barely suppress a laugh. She knew I didn't really mean it.

I actually did think about Christian a bit that afternoon, but more about his words than anything else. Specifically, the stuff about beef. I planned to discuss it with my family at dinner. I didn't expect much support, but that wasn't going to stop me.

When Aliya's mom dropped me off, I walked toward Don's house so I could grab his mail. I pulled some paper and a pen out of my backpack and scratched out a quick note to leave in the kitchen:

Mr. Francis,
Everything is fine at your house. But it misses
you. So do we.
Get well soon!
Love, Mia

Chapter

Mom nudged open the front door with her left hip, while carrying her work bag on her left shoulder and two pizza boxes in her right hand. The amazing smell of pizza lured me out of my room in a hypnotic sort of way. It was 6:10 that evening. Nate was busy doing his homework, while I had been reading articles on my phone about beef and its impact on climate change.

"I've got pizza! Why don't you guys come and eat before it gets cold. Your father will be home soon."

She didn't have to tell me twice. Nate either. And soon after we sat down, Dad arrived just in time for a family dinner. He inhaled deep.

"Can't beat the smell of pizza," he said gleefully.

I knew that I had recently alienated my family by criticizing them about their response—or lack thereof—to climate change. So I had rehearsed in my head how I would address this whole beef issue.

"So," I began after Dad sat down with us, "I learned some interesting stuff at our first Climate Club meeting today."

"Oh yeah?" replied Mom. "Like what?"

"Well, I was surprised to find out that one of the main causes of climate change is beef."

Dad and Nate stopped chewing their food and looked at each other.

"Huh?" Nate said.

I went on. "Yeah. Forests get burned down so cows have land to graze on. So those trees can't hold carbon anymore. And so much food is needed to feed the cows. Did you know there's like a billion cows in the world?"

Dad was in disbelief. "Let me get this straight. This climate thing you're doing, they're telling you to stop eating beef?"

"No. But my science teacher doesn't eat beef. She's a vegan."

I looked at everyone. Mom was listening intently. Dad, meanwhile, seemed annoyed. And to Nate, it was pretty much a joke, which initially didn't bother me because to me, he was pretty much a joke.

"I was doing some research when I got home," I continued. "When cows burp, they give off a green-house gas that's worse than carbon dioxide. It's helping to make the planet warmer."

"Bah-ha-ha!" Nate could barely control himself. "Cow burps? Cow burps? She wants us to give up steak because of *cow burps!*"

I blocked out the noise and focused on Mom, who seemed genuinely interested.

"Mom, this is serious. This kid at school today was talking about his family in Brazil, and how the Amazon rainforest is getting cut down. There are so many cows there, and it's so that people around the world can eat them. Doesn't this bother you?"

By this point, Dad and Nate were quiet.

"I've always thought we eat too much meat in this house," Mom said. "We can cut down. We'd all be better off."

Yes! A small victory! Maybe Mom was coming around to my side.

I smiled. Nate didn't.

"Because of the burps?" he hollered.

"Listen," Dad said, "I'm having my burgers, and I'm having my steak. I'm not giving that up because her science teacher says beef is bad for the planet."

I could feel some anger welling up inside me, but before I said anything, Mom jumped in: "First of all, I cook most of the meals, and I don't see that changing anytime soon. And second, nobody said anything about giving it up. But we can cut back a little."

"Thanks, Mom," I said with genuine sincerity. I looked at her. "I'd actually like to stop eating beef. So if it's okay, when you're making beef for dinner, I'll just make myself some pasta or mac and cheese or something."

"We'll figure something out," she said. "I certainly won't stop you from giving up beef, as long as you eat a healthy alternative."

This was a big moment. I thought I might be able to secure an ally in the house.

That night before bed, I opened up a notebook and began to write back to Hector. I told him about the Climate Club, picking up Don's mail, and other things going on at school. I expressed interest in reading his stories when he finished and encouraged him to keep working at it. Then I asked about a part of his letter that I couldn't quite shake: "What is this oil thing you guys are protesting?"

I tucked the letter into an envelope and copied down his address from the letter he had sent to me. Then I climbed into bed, but before closing my eyes, I texted Uncle James a question that had popped into my head after the Climate Club meeting.

"Uncle James, you said you're a vegetarian, right?"

"I try to be," he replied.

"Is it because of climate change?"

"Partly."

"How come you didn't tell me that was a reason?"

"Lol, you were mad enough already. I didn't want to make it worse."

I responded with an angry-face emoji.

"Good night, Mimi. Love you!"

"Wait!" I replied. "Hector wrote to me. Said something about a protest. Oil. What's that about?"

"Not sure. Haven't heard anything."

"OK. Goodnight." I placed my phone on the end table and tried to fall asleep.

Chapter

Things were going pretty well for me in seventh grade, I have to be honest. I really liked the four teachers on my team, and only one of my enrichment teachers was mean. That was Mr. Thompson, who taught general music.

Rebecca agreed with my assessment of Mr. Thompson. "I know, right?" she said. "Chill, dude. I don't know what Swan Lake is, no matter how much you yell at me."

"I know it's a ballet," Ariana said, "and I still think he's mean. I was like thirty seconds late to class the other day, and I thought he was gonna throw a whiteboard marker at me."

"Oh don't worry, have you seen how thick his glasses are?" Rebecca said. "He couldn't hit you with a marker if you were two feet away from him."

And then there were these strange notes that would still show up in my locker sometimes. The latest read, "I really want to get to know you."

I wished I could have written back: "I really want to get to know *who you are*."

"Besides Matt O'Connor, do you ever notice anyone looking at you a lot?" Rebecca asked.

"I don't think so," I said.

"Is there anyone who, like, never looks at you? Like someone who might be too afraid to look at you because they might be blinded by your stunning beauty?"

I rolled my eyes at her obvious sarcasm.

"No, but really, what boy hardly ever looks at you?" she asked.

"I don't know," I said. "Probably all of them! I wouldn't know because I never look at *them*."

"Maybe it's time you start," Ariana chimed in.

"It's hopeless, Ari," Rebecca said.

We all cracked up. Aliya protectively put her around me. "Leave Mia alone," she joked.

Despite how much I liked seventh grade, however, I was having one little problem at school. I guess it was a problem, though I think it was other people who had the problems. Basically, when I saw people clearly doing harm to the environment, I sometimes told them. And they didn't necessarily like it.

One such incident came the Monday after the Climate Club meeting, which was an unseasonably warm, early-October day. When I walked from the bus into the school that morning, I immediately noticed how cold it felt. Way colder than it was outside. Obviously, the air conditioning was on.

Yes, it was warm for October. But it wasn't ninety degrees! Annoyed, I poked my head into the main office on my way to homeroom. I shouldn't have done this. But it was like I couldn't stop myself.

"I know it's a little warm," I said to the secretaries—and one of the assistant principals—who were in the room. I almost couldn't believe the words were coming out of my mouth. "But air conditioning uses so much electricity. It's terrible for the planet."

One of the secretaries looked at the other, who somewhat sheepishly said, "I have a health condition, and it can be hard for me to breathe when it's too humid. So they put the AC on downstairs for me."

"Oh," I said, completely mortified. "Sorry, Mrs. Carson."

Then Mr. Jones, the assistant principal in the room, added sternly, "I'm quite sure that's none of your business, Mia." I wanted to crawl into a hole.

But I obviously didn't completely learn my lesson, because on another occasion, heading to the bus after school, I saw a seventh-grade boy named Joey open a Snickers bar and toss the wrapper on the ground.

I was so mad that I reflexively yelled at him, "Hey! You can't just litter like that!"

"Are you serious?" he shot back, surprising me with his anger. "This isn't your stupid little club. Mind your own business!"

I normally would have backed down at that point. Confrontations make me jittery. But things like littering and recycling had brought out a combative side of me that few people typically witnessed. So, channeling my inner Rebecca, I snapped, "Mind my own business? So you own the school now?"

As Joey abruptly stopped walking and turned around, Christian appeared from a group of students nearby.

"Relax, Joey," he said. "You know you'd get in

trouble if a teacher saw you do that. Just pick it up and throw it out."

"If it's so important to you guys, then maybe *you* should throw it out," Joey said. The fact that his response triggered a memory of Nate saying something similar did not help to alleviate my annoyance.

Then Joey left with his friend, Matt O'Connor— yes, *that* Matt O'Connor—at his side. As the boys walked away, I heard Matt mutter, "She's done that to me before, too. She thinks she's the friggin' recycling police."

I looked at Christian. "Thanks for helping me."

"No problem. So aggravating when people do stuff like that, right?"

"Extremely. Like they can just do whatever they want."

"You gotta be careful, though," he warned me. "He was pretty mad."

"I know. Sometimes I feel like I blurt these things out before I think about whether I should actually say them."

Christian and I were now regularly stopping to chat in the hallway, including one time when Christian's math teacher scolded us for ignoring the bell. I was learning more about him. For example, he loved soccer, and the highlight of his year so far had been a successful audition for the school's jazz band.

And he revealed that one time he had seen me play basketball. One night in January, he had gone to watch his eighth-grade cousin's team play the game after mine, so he caught the end of my game.

"You scored the game-winning basket with five seconds left," he said.

"I remember that game," I said with a smile.

"Thank you all for coming to our second meeting," Mr. Walker said one late-October Wednesday, three weeks after our first gathering. "And by the looks of it, the first meeting was a success. Good news spreads!"

This time, thirty students attended, including six new faces. Mr. Walker had to retrieve a pair of desks from the room next door so that everyone could sit. I noticed a smile was growing on my face, which felt a little embarrassing, so I lightly bit the inside of my cheeks to reign it in. But this was a good sign. Our little club just might make a difference!

The meeting's goal, Mr. Walker said, was to brainstorm ideas for how the Climate Club could take action. He instructed us to work in groups to produce a list that we could share.

I turned my desk toward Rebecca, Aliya, and Ariana, who simultaneously rotated theirs in my direction. I noticed Ariana's eyes looking over my left shoulder, so I turned my head. Standing beside us were Christian and his friend, Conor.

"Can we join you?" Christian asked.

"Sure!" I exclaimed.

As the word left my mouth, I realized that I sounded way too enthusiastic. Real smooth, Mia. My friends gave each other fleeting glances, afraid that prolonged eye contact would cause them to burst into laughter.

The six of us discussed many ideas and ended with a list of five actions. Mr. Walker and Mrs. Young stood at the whiteboard, ready to record the work of all groups. Students began sharing:

Plant trees at school
Hang posters in the hallways
Get facts read in the morning announcements
Ban plastic bottles
Make meat illegal
Get the school to turn the heat down
Detentions for littering
Skip school and protest

The last one sparked uproarious laughter.

We decided that for now, we would hang posters and strongly encourage students to bring reusable water bottles.

"Remember," Mr. Walker said, "we have a really important message here. But how we convey that message matters. People don't like to feel like they're being lectured or told that they're bad people doing bad things. The world has functioned in a certain way for a very long time. It's a system that pollutes and wastes, and we've all grown up in that system. It would be great to convince them all to change their ways, but it's really the system that needs to be changed."

Why hadn't someone told me that a few weeks earlier?

The teachers then asked us if we had any personal stories about climate change, other than what we had all recently experienced with Reggie.

Yes. Hector. I raised my hand.

"I went to Chicago in September when we were out of school," I said. "And I met a kid there from East City, Indiana. He has asthma and lead poisoning, or something like that. School is hard for him sometimes. He almost died once from an asthma attack.

It's apparently from all the pollution there. He's such a nice kid. I feel so bad. My uncle says he'll deal with that for his whole life."

When I finished, I noticed Mrs. Young looking right at me and nodding, as if she knew Hector personally. Then, about ten seconds later, she said, "I hate hearing stories like that." It sounded like there was a lump in her throat.

"But I know, Mia, that there are so many people like your friend, people who are affected by pollution and climate change. And there's gonna be more. Which is why we have to do something."

She took a deep breath before telling us something pretty unexpected.

"You guys are all eleven, twelve, thirteen years old. When you were born, climate change was even less focused on than it is now. I just had my first baby a few months ago. And I'll be honest, I thought a lot about whether to bring a child into this world that's getting hotter, more unstable, and where so many people seem not to care. Is it fair to that child?"

I was beginning to understand why Mrs. Young called climate change "personal."

She continued, "And I don't talk about this much in class because I know I'll get emotional and angry. But that's why I make sure I can be part of these meetings. This is an important topic for me. I've really struggled with it. I want our kids to be as happy as they can be."

The pin-drop silence that followed Mrs. Young's words was interrupted by an announcement on the intercom that it was time for students taking late buses to meet outside.

"Okay, the next meeting will be in three weeks," Mr. Walker said. "See you all later."

I said goodbye to Christian. Then I walked over to my friends.

"Let's go talk to Mrs. Young," I said.

Rebecca and Aliya agreed.

"Make it quick," said Ariana, who was not one of Mrs. Young's students. "I have things to do."

"Please, no you don't," Rebecca said. "You never have anything to do."

We smiled, but our smiles quickly faded as we approached our teacher.

"Hi Mrs. Young," I said softly.

"Hey girls."

"Are you sure you're okay?" Rebecca asked.

"Yeah. Thanks for asking."

There was a brief moment of silence as we seemed to wait for someone to ask the question that was on all of our minds. Finally, Aliya spoke up. "Do you really think it's going to be that bad? For future generations?"

"I hope not," Mrs. Young said. "I really hope not."

"But what you said," Rebecca said, "that you weren't sure if you wanted to have a baby because of climate change?"

"Well, I thought a lot about it, for sure. My husband and I talked about it quite a bit. And we decided, ultimately, that if we could raise our daughter the right way, maybe she could help to make a difference. Like what you all are doing now in this club."

Mrs. Young's words, her emotion, left me a bit shaken. For my whole life, the adults around me had rarely even mentioned climate change. But now,

Mrs. Young was telling us that she was concerned for my generation.

"Do you think there's a chance to fix the climate?" I asked her.

She paused, seeming to search her mind for the right words.

"Yes and no," she said. "The reality is, some of the damage is already done. When summer sea ice melts, for example, that's not coming back in our lifetimes. Sea levels are rising. They won't just go back down."

Those words gave me a queasy feeling.

"But," she added, "there's definitely a chance to make this a better world. People have disrupted nature for centuries now. We live in a world with air pollution, water pollution, oil drilling, burning forests. But imagine if that all changed. Even in a warmer world, if it became a better place, where people respected nature instead of trying to control it, and the air was cleaner because we planted more trees and stopped burning dirty fuels—I'd love to raise a child in a world like that."

I thought about what she said for the rest of the day. It was depressing and inspiring at the same time. But it made me more determined than ever. For the sake of myself and my friends, for Mrs. Young's baby daughter, and for my own future children and grandchildren, I needed to do something.

I wasn't sure exactly what to do. But it had to be something big.

"Hey Mia, can I have your phone number?" Christian asked me one day as we were the first two to sit at our lunch table. Christian and Conor had been eating with us for about a week or so.

I wasn't sure how to respond, and I was kind of embarrassed.

"Um, okay," I said.

I didn't know how to interpret his motive. Having a phone was still new to me, and other than family members, only girls' numbers were in my contacts. Christian could sense my hesitation.

"Our math teachers do the same things every day," he said. "One of my friends is on your team, and the work is the exact same. I thought maybe we could do homework together sometimes, or text about it."

I exhaled and then chuckled. "Are you bad at math and you want my help?" I joked.

"Yeah, I figured you could text me all the answers while I watch soccer."

Naturally, Rebecca arrived at the table as the phone numbers were being exchanged.

"Sooo," she said with a wide grin on her face, "what's going on here?"

I avoided eye contact with my friend. "Nothing you need to worry about."

When Ariana and Aliya showed up, Rebecca turned to them and said, "This thing where Mia and Christian are exchanging numbers? That's nothing we need to worry about. Just letting you guys know."

Without looking up, I could tell how much the three of them were enjoying all of this.

"Conor, were you aware of this whole situation?" Rebecca asked him as he sat down with his lunch tray.

"Yeah, Christian told me he was gonna ask for her number," he said. Christian glared at him, though he did crack a slight smile.

Conor continued, talking more quietly than before but loud enough that I heard. "It's no big surprise. He talks about her a lot."

He talks about me a lot? But I didn't talk about him at all. I was too afraid my friends would make fun of me. But I did *think* about him. What did that mean? It was nice to hear that Christian talked about me, but I was definitely confused by my feelings. I had always been too focused on other things to even think about boys. And whenever a girl started "seeing" some boy—including Ariana the previous spring— she seemed to get distracted from school and other important things.

I had been determined to avoid that trap. Only this felt different. I was initially drawn to Christian because of his genuine concern for the environment.

But now I could tell that our friendship was strengthening. And evolving.

A few days later, Christian and I had made plans to FaceTime and work on a challenging math homework assignment. Before that, I stopped at Don's house for my mail duties.

I carried in his mail, which included a pamphlet for army veterans, *Time* magazine, bills, and junk mail. As I held the pile over the cardboard box, I noticed something inside the box. It was an envelope with "Mia" written on the outside.

I opened the envelope. It contained a brief note from Don.

> *Mia,*
> *I appreciate you getting my mail. And your notes lift my spirits every time. Please keep them coming! You're very thoughtful.*
> *Say hi to your family.*
> *Don*
>
> *P.S. If you see any bills in the mail, you can just pay them. I don't want them!*

This cracked me up. I remembered that about a year ago, Don had traveled to visit Ben in Georgia. I was outside with Dad the day before Don left, and Don asked him to hold his mail for the week that he was away.

"You can read my magazines, if any interest you," Don had said, "and if there are any bills, keep them." I can't explain why, but I found it endearing that he had a go-to joke.

As I had done several times, I fished out paper and a pen from my backpack and wrote a response.

Mr. Francis,
Thanks for your note! I can't pay your bills. I
have like $56. I would if I could.
I'll keep sending you notes. I like writing them.
But I'd rather see you waving to me in the
morning again. I really hope you get better
soon.
Love,
Mia

I placed the note at the top of the mail pile. Then I slid Don's note in my backpack. Now I had two pen pals!

My previous pen pal, Hector, finally responded in a letter that arrived near the end of October. He included one of his short stories about a family of squirrels that lived near an apartment building and developed a bond with the people who lived there, only to save one of the boys' lives at the end. It was pretty good!

He told me that he was worried because his mom had hurt her ankle when she stumbled on a crowded train. Tracey could still work her daytime job, but she wasn't able to wait tables, and they relied on her tips.

As for the mysterious oil situation, Hector reported that his mom said she had heard rumors about the oil refinery in town, and that something was happening there. But she was unable to provide details.

I really wanted those details.

That weekend, my family drove up to Chelmsford to visit my dad's parents, my grandparents. It had been a couple of months since our last visit, and while I loved my grandparents, my Grandpa could occasionally get on my nerves. He was sometimes, let's say, loud. At least when he came to our house, especially when it was a big gathering with people he didn't know as well, he toned it down a bit.

That Sunday afternoon, nothing was toned down.

For one thing, he often seemed to speak before thinking. My fifth-grade teacher, Mrs. Windsor, had a sign on her bulletin board that read: "Engage your brain before activating your mouth." Grandpa seemed to follow that advice, only in reverse.

"Hey guys! Come on in here!" he bellowed from his living room chair as soon as we had entered the house. "About time you came out to see us!"

We all dutifully headed in to greet him, but a moment later, my grandma called to my parents from the kitchen: "Robbie and Sovannary, come see all the potatoes that we harvested this year!"

That left Nate and me sitting on the big couch with Grandpa in his recliner that no one else—not even Grandma—was allowed to sit in. He was primarily focused on the TV—he always watched the same news channel, and often when he visited our house, his first order of business was to seize the remote and find that very channel.

Nate took out his phone and started texting. "Put that phone away!" Grandpa said. "Your generation, always glued to your electronics." He seemed not to notice, or care, that he said those words without looking away from his electronic TV.

Then a story came on the news about climate change. The segment focused on a protest taking place in South Dakota against an underground oil pipeline, where oil was traveling from Canada to different parts of the United States. But the newscasters actually mocked the protesters! They even interviewed someone who listed several reasons why he felt the protesters were wrong.

This annoyed me. And then Grandpa offered his own commentary on the story, which only added to my agitation. "Can you believe this nonsense? These clowns are trying to stop us from using oil. How do they think that will all turn out?"

Normally, I was deferential around adults who weren't my parents. But this time, Grandpa had struck a nerve. "Grandpa, oil is destroying the planet."

"Oh, don't tell me they've got you believing this crap."

"It's not crap."

I didn't want to fight with him, but I had heard him ridicule the concept of recycling over the years ("I'm not cleaning my trash so it can go in a different bucket") and snap at Grandma when she suggested he not water the grass daily during a summer heat wave ("I want a green lawn. There's plenty of water to go around"). Perhaps this battle had been brewing.

"You're just a kid," he said, shaking his head. "The world is a complicated place."

"Grandpa, you watch the news. Haven't you heard about sea levels rising? Droughts? Wildfires? The planet's getting warmer. Because of us."

Grandpa huffed. Then he responded to me as if he was some expert. "That's all made up. You sound like your Uncle James."

I considered that a compliment.

"Politicians are selling him this stuff so he'll vote for them," Grandpa said. "He's made the oil companies into the bad guys. I got news for you—we ain't surviving without oil."

I considered letting it go, but I was in too deep. "What about Reggie?" I asked.

"What about it? There have been hurricanes forever. It has nothing to do with global warming or climate change or whatever they're calling it now."

"But the storms are worse now, Grandpa. And it's because of us. We don't need oil. Nobody *needs* oil. It's not like there's been cars and electricity forever."

The volume of Grandpa's voice climbed. "What's next, you're gonna tell me that we can't go on airplanes anymore? Or that cows are evil? I've heard this stuff before. It's a joke! This is what those politicians want people to think. Then you'll all get scared and vote for them."

"Grandpa, airplanes use a lot of fuel. And forests get cut down for cows. That stuff isn't a joke."

Grandpa looked at Nate, seemingly seeking his support. But Nate had been gradually sinking into the sofa as if he might disappear into the cushions to dodge the discomfort of the moment. I was pleasantly surprised that Nate hadn't piled on with Grandpa. And I wasn't pleasantly surprised with Nate very often.

I softened my voice and tried to appeal to the side of my Grandpa that used to hand me Hershey's Kisses and Twizzler's whenever I came to his house. "Don't you care about my future, Grandpa?"

Instead, this set him off.

"Of course I do!"

Grandma and my parents finally responded to the commotion from that outburst. But Grandpa wasn't done.

"*I* actually do care. I care that you get to live in a great country like I have. The *greatest* country. And a country where we put hideous windmills all over the place, and everyone's charging their little electric cars, and China is running circles around us—that's not the country my grandchildren should grow up in. I don't want anybody telling me I can't use oil, or get on a plane, or eat a burger. That's not the future I want for my grandchildren."

Dad mercifully interjected. "Okay, I think this conversation should probably end here."

"Your daughter has a lot to learn," Grandpa said as he got up and stormed out of the room.

The visit that day was briefer than normal. We had a big ham and potatoes lunch that Grandma had prepared, but conversation was limited. Soon after, we left.

About fifteen minutes of silence began the car ride home before I finally spoke. I needed to say something. I felt like I was at least partially responsible for ruining our afternoon.

"I'm sorry, Dad. I shouldn't have argued with Grandpa. I feel bad about it."

"It's okay," he said. "I've had my own battles with him over the years. Plus, he's the adult. He needs to act like one."

Nate laughed. "Don't do that to me again, Mia. That was so awkward. I wanted to die."

Chapter

I noticed that our car pulled off the highway unexpectedly about halfway home from my grandparents' house that afternoon.

"Where are we going, Dad?" I asked.

"You'll see."

He eventually pulled into the parking lot of a fairly large, one-story building.

"What is this place?" asked Nate, glancing up from his phone and seeming to just realize that the car was no longer traveling seventy miles per hour.

"This is the rehab facility where Don is staying. I thought we could say hello."

We're visiting Don? I felt somewhat nervous because I knew he'd want to talk to me, and I wanted to be able to say more than just "Hi" and "Good." After all the little notes I had written to him, I'd look really dumb if I hid behind my parents and barely spoke.

Our visit was definitely a surprise to him.

"Hi, Don!" Dad said when we entered his room.

It took him a couple of seconds to respond. He seemed in disbelief.

"Hey guys! Wow! I had no idea you were coming! What a great surprise! Sorry you have to see me like this."

"Who are they, Don?" asked the nurse in his room. "You better introduce me to this fine-looking family."

"These are my neighbors." Don quickly told the nurse all of our names. He may have been eighty-six and had two damaged legs, but his mind remained sharp.

"Wait a minute," the nurse said, "this is Mia. *The* Mia?"

Uh-oh. Unwanted attention alert.

"Mia from these letters?" The nurse turned toward Don's end table, revealing the little pile of notes I had written to him.

Nate looked at me with a confused face. "You've been writing to him all this time?"

"Yeah, Nate," Don said. Then he smiled. "What about you? Too busy for me?"

Nate laughed, but he turned a little red. I suspected that the problem wasn't that Nate had been ignoring Don; the thought of writing to our elderly neighbor had probably just never occurred to him.

Then I told myself that it was time to start acting my age and speak to my neighbor—my friend—confidently.

"How are you feeling, Mr. Francis?"

"Hey, call me Don," he said. "Just like I always tell you. In your notes, too. No more Mr. Francis, you got that?"

"Okay. How are you feeling, Don?"

He was beaming. "I'm feeling great. Especially now!"

Mom looked at the nurse. "How's he coming along?"

"He's doing pretty good. Good days and bad. That was a pretty traumatic experience for those old legs. But they're healing and we're looking forward to when he can start his rehab."

"I'm looking forward to when I can do anything," Don said. "At home I was always doing something. In the house, or around the yard. I've already read these books my daughter brought for me."

He pointed to two history books, plus a third, which forcefully grabbed my attention. It was called *Half Earth: Our Planet's Fight For Life.*

"She's bringing me some more this week," he added. "The Red Sox season is over, and the Patriots only play once a week. So I'm bored a lot."

"Bored?" the nurse said, pretending to be incredulous. "As much talking as you do? When are you ever bored?"

"That's what I do when I'm bored!" he fired back. "I start talking to you guys."

The nurse smiled, shook her head, and walked out of the room. "I'll let you guys catch up."

We stayed for about an hour, probably longer than Dad had anticipated, but like the nurse said, Don loved to talk. He told some stories, asked Nate and me about school, and expressed his displeasure with that common enemy: Reggie.

Then, regarding the hurricane, he said something that the others seemed not to really notice. But I sure did.

"I guess sometimes we reap what we sow."

Did he mean that by altering the climate with so many fossil fuels, we had brought the storm on ourselves? I wanted to ask him to clarify. But Dad had clearly started the process toward leaving, so I held onto my thought.

We were saying our goodbyes when Don called me over.

"I really want to thank you again for getting my mail and writing those wonderful notes."

"Oh, I am happy to get your mail. And I like writing the notes. I loved getting yours. It's like we're pen pals now."

Don reached over to his end table and grabbed a piece of paper.

"The nurse brought this to me just before you got here. So keep checking. Your next letter will be soon."

"Great! And you keep checking. I'll keep writing."

Don smiled.

"See you later," I said. And suddenly, unexpectedly, I found myself leaning over to hug Don. It seemed to surprise him at first, too, but then he embraced me back.

I waved as I walked away from his bedside.

"Bye, Don!" we all said. "Great to see ya."

"Bye," he said. Then he looked toward me and softly said, "Thank you."

As October turned into November, I continued to focus my attention on climate change, at school and home. I regularly chatted and texted with Christian about ways to act greener in our own lives. And I noticed that Mom was cooking beef less often; Asian dishes with rice or noodles were finding their way to the dinner table with increasing frequency.

I also managed to get two promises from Dad—he would look into solar panels for our roof, and he agreed to set up a clothesline in the backyard. I had read that dryers used a lot of electricity, which led to a tricky conversation, given Dad's profession. But he, perhaps looking to avoid another battle with me about climate change, responded positively to the idea.

In mid-November, the Climate Club met for the third time, and it was so much fun. We designed posters and walked around the school to hang them up. My poster included a cow and some trees, with the words: "Eating beef kills forests. And cows." I delighted in hanging it right outside the cafeteria to really make my point.

I stood beside Christian as he secured his poster to the wall, and I noticed that he had included the hashtag #FridaysForFuture in the bottom-right corner.

"What's that?" I asked, pointing to the hashtag.

"Oh. It's a hashtag for student climate protests that gets used on Twitter."

"Really? Student protests?" My interest was piqued.

"Yeah. They have them all over the world on Fridays. Students protest at government buildings or outside of schools. It's pretty big, I guess."

When I got home that afternoon, I was alone, which was normal, and I immediately sat on the couch and opened the laptop that my parents shared. I went to Twitter, the social media website.

Mom's account came up, already signed in. I typed #FridaysForFuture in the search bar. After I pressed enter, an endless stream of posts with that hashtag appeared on the screen.

I scrolled through them. I saw photo after photo from country upon country. Students of all races holding signs:

Climate Emergency

Protect Our Future

There Is No Planet B

Our House Is On Fire

I could barely blink. I had often felt so alone on this issue. So few people seemed to understand my concern, and many of them thought it was basically a joke. Now I saw kids around the globe who obviously cared about climate change and were turning that into action. I was overcome with a desire to join them. To participate.

I continued scrolling until I spotted a post that brought me to a screeching halt:

Climate protest at #Boston state capitol. Friday at 10 am. We need a big turnout to send a message. Our future is at stake. #Fridaysforfuture

Friday? Boston? That was only forty miles away. I had to go. But I knew Mom and Dad would never let me go. No chance. They had to work and wouldn't be able to take me, even if they wanted to. There was no way I'd be allowed to go.

But I had to go.

"I'm gonna go," I told my friends during lunch on Thursday.

"How?" Aliya asked. "How would you even get there?"

"Train. I'll take my bike to the train station. I already looked up the schedule. It's not that hard. I've taken the train with my family before from Plymouth to Boston."

As I talked, I think I was trying to convince myself that I could do it. But I really wanted company. The idea of going alone was kind of scary.

"So will any of you come with me?"

"I would, Mia, but it seems crazy," Ariana said.

"There's no way," Aliya said. "If I got caught, I'd get in so much trouble."

Rebecca appeared to be considering it, like she was trying to will herself to say yes.

"C'mon, Becks," I pleaded.

"You know I'd do just about anything for you." Rebecca sighed. "But I'm already in trouble. My parents took away my phone because of my math and English test grades. I can't *skip school* now to go to a climate protest."

I sighed. But I understood. I probably would have said no, too. Then I heard a voice.

"I'll go."

It was Christian. He had just sat down.

"What?" I didn't know what else to say.

"You're talking about the protest in Boston?"

"Yeah."

"Okay. I'll go with you. I want to go."

"Are you sure?"

"Yes! Do you not *want* me to go?"

"No, I do. It would be great. But ..."

I had already considered how my parents might react if they discovered that I skipped school and went to Boston with Rebecca, Aliya, or Ariana. They'd be furious, but at least they knew those girls and their parents.

But they had never met Christian. They had never *heard* of him.

And he was a boy. The thought terrified me. My parents might lock me in my room for the rest of middle school.

On the other hand, I liked Christian. A lot. And it would make me feel much safer if I wasn't alone. It would also be more fun.

"But what?" Christian asked.

I relented. "If you're okay going, I'd love for you to come."

After school, on the bus ride home, Aliya tried to talk me out of going to the protest.

"You've never been to the city without grownups,

Mia. And aren't your parents gonna find out? How could they not find out?"

I listened, but my mind was made up.

"I really wanna do this," I said. "This is so important. I feel like I have to get involved and do something."

"You are. You basically started a whole club about it at school. What more can you do? You're in seventh grade!"

"Well, age doesn't matter. Older people aren't really doing anything. And it's our generation that will be messed up from all this."

Aliya backed down. She knew I wasn't going to be talked out of it.

When I got home, I called Christian. Mom occasionally checked my texts just to make sure I was using the phone appropriately. If my plans with Christian were in my text message log, I'd be caught red-handed. We agreed to meet at the train station around 8:30 the next morning. The train was scheduled to depart at 8:45.

With my backpack in hand, I walked toward the front door about ten minutes earlier than normal the following morning. Only Mom was still home.

"You're heading out early," she noted.

"Yeah. I'm gonna take my bike to Aliya's and get on the bus there." I had prepared that lie in advance. "We're gonna work on our social studies project together after school."

"The one about the Egyptian pharaohs?"

"Yeah."

"On a Friday?"

"We want to get a head start on it so we're not rushing at the end."

"Well that sounds smart. All right, see you this evening. Love you."

"Bye, Mom. Love you too."

Phew. I got away with that one.

I walked through the damp, dewy grass to the shed in the backyard and took out my bike. I fastened my helmet to my head and started to ride away, making sure to take a route that would not cross paths with the bus. Then I avoided the main roads on my way to the Plymouth commuter rail station.

I arrived at 8:20 and waited patiently as five minutes passed. Then ten. At 8:35, I was starting to panic. Did Christian get caught? Did he decide to bail? Two minutes later, to my relief, I spotted him zipping into the parking lot.

"Sorry I'm late," he said, panting. "It wasn't easy getting out, so I waited till the bus was gone. I hid in the backyard until my dad left with my sister for her before-school program."

"It's okay. You made it. The train leaves in like eight minutes. I got my ticket, but you need to get yours."

Christian quickly paid for his ticket and we boarded the train. It would take us to South Station, where we would connect to the Red Line. We expected to arrive at the Statehouse by 10:15 or so, only missing a few minutes of the protest.

On the train, we made signs to hold up at the protest. We also talked. A lot.

It became clear how much Christian loved his little sister, Maria. And I learned that he had fallen off his bike and broken his arm when he was in second grade, and it took almost two years before he was willing to get back on the bike.

I told him that I really wished I had a younger sister, that I loved little kids and hoped to one day have a career that allowed me to work with them.

"Like an elementary school teacher?" Christian asked.

"I don't know. Maybe. Or pediatrician, or a nurse at a children's hospital. Something like that. What about you?"

"You mean, when I'm done with my pro soccer career in Europe?"

I rolled my eyes and laughed.

"Oh yeah, I forgot that I'll be the starting point guard for the Celtics first," I joked. "Then something with kids."

As the train arrived at the station in Boston, I stuffed my phone back into my backpack. We got off the train and began briskly walking toward the Beacon Hill area in Boston. The weather was pretty warm considering Thanksgiving was in less than two weeks; that fact, unfortunately, seemed to fit the theme of the day.

When the Statehouse was in sight, we noticed several dozen people gathered in front of it, many holding signs. Almost all of them appeared to be high school students. We lengthened our strides so we could get there more quickly.

The protest was very calm. No yelling. No speakers. It was a sit-in. Several students took pictures, which we did our best to avoid. Same for the TV news camera that got there around 10:45. The last thing we needed was to turn up on the local news.

We sat down and were greeted enthusiastically by those around us, like we were now part of a community. A community of climate warriors.

"It's great that you guys are here! I'm Tess and this is Ava. Where are you guys from?"

"Plymouth. I'm Christian."

"I'm Mia. Nice to meet you."

Ava told us that she and Tess had initiated a program at their high school to reduce trash, especially in the cafeteria. They convinced their principal to start a compost pile on school grounds.

"It makes me crazy to see people just throw things away. So wasteful."

"Not to mention the methane," Tess said.

I had crammed a lot of facts into my brain in recent weeks, and Tess's comment triggered something in my memory. "Methane? Isn't that from cows?"

"Yes! But also all that trash in the landfills creates methane gas. It's terrible for the environment. Stronger than carbon dioxide."

"We started a Climate Club at our middle school," Christian said. "Well, basically Mia started it."

"Awesome!" Ava said.

Then Tess asked an obvious question.

"How did you guys get here?"

"We took the train," I said.

"From Plymouth? Your parents were okay with that?"

Christian and I smiled sheepishly but didn't say anything.

Ava put two and two together. "Ohhhh."

"Well," said Tess, "we're from Newton. We know the area and the T pretty well. You can stick with us."

The T was what locals called the train system, similar to the L in Chicago.

"Yeah," said Ava, "let us know if you need anything."

Christian and I sensed an opportunity to pick the brains of these older girls.

"Have you been to any of these protests before?" Christian asked.

"A few," replied Tess.

"My brother goes to college in Washington D.C., and he's very involved," Ava said. "Him and his friends go to places where politicians give talks, and they ask them questions about climate change. He's even picketed outside of Congress."

I found myself surprised by that. "I thought hardly anyone cared about climate change. I barely ever heard about it before the hurricane, and even then, I was looking it up online. Like no one I know seems to care about it at all."

"You guys do," Tess said.

"Well yeah. But that's two people."

Tess nodded. "Okay. So you'll find more in high school, I'm sure. I agree that it seems most older people couldn't care less. But it's our future that could be really messed up, and there are protests like this all over the world."

"Yeah," I said, "I kind of noticed that when I went on Twitter the other day." Still, this begged the obvious question, which I asked. "Is anything actually getting done because of the protests?"

"A little bit," Ava said.

"But the oil companies will do anything to stop it," Tess said, rolling her eyes in disgust, "and they have more money than God."

"My brother says the oil companies have known for a long time how bad the climate was getting, but they lied to everyone," Ava said. "And they give all this money to politicians. So they've always had the votes they've needed."

"So how do we beat them?" Christian asked.

"I don't know," Tess said, "but we can't give up, that's for sure. I just hope that as more people get on our side, who are willing to protest and things like that, that eventually we'll win."

"But it has to happen soon," Ava said. "The longer it takes, the worse the climate gets."

Christian and I looked at each other, seemingly unsure whether to be inspired or defeated by our conversation with Ava and Tess. It wasn't the first time I had felt that way.

We chatted with other students around us as well. One girl, a sophomore from Boston named Destiny, said she sometimes felt depressed about what the planet might look like when she reached her thirties or forties.

"I always figured I would want to be a mom," she said. "But now I'm not so sure."

We told Destiny about Mrs. Young, and why she eventually decided to have a baby.

"Maybe I'll feel that way when I'm older," she said. "I don't know."

The best part of the day was just the rush of adrenaline I felt from being part of this movement. At times, Christian and I exchanged glances that seemed to say, *Can you believe we're actually doing this?* I knew I couldn't sit idly by anymore. I had learned too much about climate change. The urge to be involved had grown so strong.

At about 11:00, a well-dressed woman walked out from the Statehouse to address the crowd.

"The governor appreciates why you're here, and he shares your concerns. Climate change is at the top of his agenda. He is working on an emissions-reduction bill right now that he plans to submit to the legislature by the end of the year. He thanks you for your support on this issue. Have a good day."

"That's their way of saying they want us to leave now," a boy near us was saying. "But we're not going. Not for a while. Until we make our point."

Just then, I heard my phone vibrate in my backpack. My heart sank. I took out the phone, looked at the cover screen, and audibly gasped.

"What's wrong?" Christian asked.

"I have so many messages from my mom. And my dad. Missed calls, too. They're worried. This is bad."

"How would they even know?"

Then, suddenly, there was a familiar voice behind us.

"There you are!"

My head whipped around. "Mom! What are you doing here?"

"Excuse me, what are *you* doing here?"

Chapter

My mom, clearly furious at me, had just found me at the climate protest and removed me from it. In front of all of these high school kids. It was the most embarrassing moment of my life. By far.

"How did you know I was here?" I asked her.

By now, the three of us were walking away from the crowd.

"Your phone, Mia. I can track your phone."

She can track my phone. Right. Crap.

Then Mom abruptly stopped walking. She looked at Christian sternly.

"And who are you?"

"Christian."

"He's in the Climate Club with me," I said, trying to save him from my mom's wrath.

"Do your parents know you're here?"

"No."

"Can you please give me one of their numbers? I'll drive you home, but I'm going to call them later. I want to make sure they know what happened today. I'd want to know."

We resumed walking until we reached the car in a nearby parking garage. It took about an hour to drive home. Not a word was spoken for the entire ride to Christian's house. Not one.

After we dropped him off, that changed.

"I want you to know," Mom started, "that I've never been more worried about anything in my life. The school called to find out why you were absent. I knew you had taken your bike. I worried that you had been kidnapped or something."

"I'm sorry, Mom, but—"

"But nothing! I'm not done." Mom shot me a devastating look. She was as mad as I had ever seen her.

"So I texted you and called you. Nothing. Put yourself in my shoes at that moment. My baby is mysteriously not at school when I watched her leave the house for school. Then she's not responding to my messages. Do you know what was going through my head? Can you even imagine?"

"No." I hung my head, unwilling to make eye contact with her. Of course I knew that if I got caught, I'd be in trouble. I just didn't think I'd get caught.

"So I had to leave work to go get you," Mom continued. "I know now that you went to a climate change protest. I know that matters to you, that you care about that. But to go to the city alone? Did you ride your bike to the train station? That's a couple of miles from home. And did you think about what can happen to a twelve-year-old girl who's alone in a big city?"

"I wasn't alone. Christian was with me."

That didn't help my cause. After I said it, I thought fire might shoot out of Mom's eyes.

"That's another thing. Who is he? How well do you even know him? You skipped school to go to Boston with some *boy*?"

"He's one of my really good friends."

"Really good friends? I've never heard of him, Mia! Not once!"

"I just met him this year. But he's in the Climate Club with us, and he really cares about climate change."

"Was this all his idea?"

"No, no. It was mine. He offered to come."

"Okay, but how well do you know him? Do you know his family?"

"I know him. He has a little sister. He plays the saxophone. And he's great. He's not like one of those boys who just talks about video games all the time. He's really caring."

Mom furrowed her brow.

"He's not...." She paused. I had no idea what she was trying to say.

"Not what?"

"He's not your boyfriend, is he?"

What?! "No, Mom! We're friends."

"Well, why did you ask him to go? You have other friends."

"I asked them. They said no."

"Oh, so they actually used their brains."

Ouch. That stung. I didn't respond.

Then Mom said, "You knew what you were doing was wrong, right? Please tell me that."

"I did. But...."

"But what?"

"I don't know. What people are doing, they're destroying our planet. That's wrong. It bothers me. Sometimes it's all I think about."

"I know, Mia. And I'm starting to understand that. I've been reading more about it, and I get why you're upset. I really do. And I'll help you, at least in our house. But you going to this protest could have put you in danger, and it will not stop climate change."

"Mom, more people need to speak up. The more of us who do, the better the chance. I feel like if I didn't go, it's like I'd be helping to make it worse. I felt like I *had* to go."

For the previous few minutes, we had been parked at the Plymouth train station. We got out of the car and retrieved my bike, which had been locked on the bike rack with several others, including Christian's. We put it into the back of our SUV.

As we began driving home, Mom discussed punishment.

"First of all, I'm going to take your phone for a while. Not sure how long yet. And when we get home, I want you to write apology letters to your teachers and the principal. Explain what you did and that you will make up the work you missed Monday night."

I rolled my eyes. Thankfully, Mom didn't notice.

"Beyond that, we'll see. I'll talk to your father tonight."

My father. Oh. I hadn't really thought about Dad.

"Does he know already?" I asked.

"Yes he does."

"Is he mad?"

"He was mostly scared. I texted him that you're okay. I'm sure by the time he gets home, he won't be too pleased."

And he wasn't, though the lecture I got from him that night was no worse than Mom's. They decided that I would lose my phone for at least two weeks. But worse than that was when they stressed that I would have to work at regaining their trust. They said it might be a while before I'm allowed to do certain things without an adult.

"We're very disappointed in you," Dad said. Not the words I wanted to hear.

While I was truly sorry to have upset Mom and Dad, I definitely didn't regret what I did. I felt part of something big. Something consequential.

On Monday, I handed my letters to Principal Lewis and all of my teachers. None of them specifically commented on it, except Mr. Walker.

"Wow," he said. "You really *do* care about this."

I just nodded. I didn't feel like talking about it.

The first time I saw Christian that day was at lunch.

"Were your parents mad?" I asked him.

"Yeah. I thought my Dad's head was gonna explode."

"Oh no. I'm so sorry."

"It's okay," he said. "It's not your fault."

"Did you get in trouble?"

"Yeah. They took my phone. And other than school and soccer and my sax lessons, I'm basically grounded for a couple of weeks. Thank God they didn't take away soccer."

Then Christian chuckled.

"What?" I asked.

"They asked me if you were my girlfriend."

I totally blushed. I could feel it. "My mom asked me if you were my boyfriend," I confessed.

I couldn't help but wonder: How did Christian answer that question?

I was sitting at my desk working on homework Monday night when I heard a knock on my bedroom door. It was Nate.

Coming to gloat, I assumed.

"Can I come in?" he asked.

"I guess."

He walked in and sat on the side of my bed. I braced myself. I expected that he would bask in my punishment.

"So Mom isn't telling me much about Friday," he said. "Only that you skipped school to go to Boston for a protest?"

"Yeah," I said in a snippy tone. "And if you came in here to harass me about it …"

"No, no. I'm just shocked. I never thought you'd do anything like that. You went to Boston by yourself. I mean, I've never done anything like *that*."

"Well, I wasn't by myself. Christian came with me."

"Whoa, wait. Did you say Kris-TEN? Or Chris-CHYEN?"

I repeated myself slightly slower. "Christian."

"You went to Boston with a boy," he said. "In seventh grade. And Mom and Dad didn't kill you?"

I could feel my blood starting to boil. "Why are you in here?"

"I just want to know why."

"Why what?"

"Why you did it. Why you skipped school to go to a climate change rally. Why you're arguing with us about recycling and eating meat. Why you're fighting with Grandpa about the news. And doing this club at school. Why is this so important to you?"

As I thought about exactly what to say, I felt my eyes welling up.

"Aw man, I wasn't trying to make you all emotional," Nate said. He started to get up from the bed.

"I don't understand why you're *not* upset about all of it," I said as I wiped under my eyes with my fingertips. "Not just you. Most people. Most people don't seem to care. Do you know that scientists think storms like Reggie, or the ones that hit Puerto Rico a couple of years ago, are because of climate change?"

"Come on, Mia. Hurricanes are from climate change?"

"Not just hurricanes. But that storms are stronger now. And it's gonna get worse. When we're older, who knows how bad it'll be? Don't you worry about what it'll be like for your family someday? And they say that poor people will suffer the most from this. Doesn't that bother you?"

Nate seemed unsure how to answer at first. "I don't know. We learned about it in school a few times. They tell us about melting ice, and it's getting warmer. But they never sound all concerned or anything."

"That's the problem!" I exclaimed. "People just go on with their lives like it's not even happening. I can't—it's just crazy!"

I faced the Chromebook I had been using and clicked on the YouTube bookmark.

"Look at this." I showed him a video titled "How Earth Would Look If All The Ice Melted." We watched as different parts of the world map appeared on the screen. As the ice melted, some cities were essentially swallowed up by the ocean. Cities like Miami and New Orleans. Others along the east coast of the United States would shrink. It was similar in other parts of the world.

Nate was momentarily frozen. Then he said, "But is all of the ice gonna melt?"

"I don't know. But some of it already is."

Then I showed him a second video, this one taken on a cell phone in Siberia, northern Russia. The area being filmed was covered in snow, but there was something odd about the snow: it was black. Soot from factories had left a light dusting on the white snow, making it look more like cookies and cream, heavy on the cookies.

I opened a third video. It showed walruses in the Arctic piling onto a small island because there was no sea ice where they could rest. Some walruses climbed up an elevated area of the island to get some space. When it was time to return to the ocean for food, the walruses, who have poor vision, threw themselves off the cliff. Many died. Their instinct was to go to the ocean, but they didn't know how to get there. None of this was normal for them.

The narrator explained that melting sea ice was causing problems like this for walruses and other animals in the Arctic.

"I read something the other day about an area in the Arctic," I said, "I think in Russia, where it was a hundred degrees one day this summer. And what about the crazy fires in California?"

I sighed. "My science teacher says it's not too late. Some of it can't be fixed, but some can. And the world can be better if we stop drilling for oil and burning coal and all that stuff."

Nate seemed taken aback. By all of it—the videos, my emotions.

"I never really thought much about it because nobody ever seemed worried," he said. "Until you. But Mom and Dad never talk about it. At school, they're still using the AC some days, and every classroom has like ninety lights on all the time. Plus, how many solar panels do you see? There's that giant windmill off the highway, and it never even does anything. It's always still! I guess I figured that if it was really serious, people would be doing stuff about it."

He paused, then added, "I guess maybe it's a bigger problem than I realized."

"Mr. Walker says people don't talk about it because if they do, it means they might have to try to fix it. And that will be hard. So people just wait around and hope the government, or some genius, will figure it out. But we all have to do something. Now. And we learned at the protest that a lot of high school and college kids are really trying. I was inspired by them."

Nate sat still for a minute, seeming to process the whole conversation. Then he stood up and started to leave the room. He turned back toward me as he approached the doorway.

"In the future," he said, "if you're gonna do

something crazy like go to Boston, can you tell me first? I'm your older brother. I might be able to help you. Instead of some random guy going with you."

"He's not random. He's my friend." I smiled a bit. "But does that mean you would have actually gone with me?"

Nate looked at me and shrugged. He walked out the door before abruptly poking his head back in.

"I forgot to tell you that you have some mail in the living room," he said.

I sped into the living room and grabbed the mail. It was from Hector. I quickly returned to my room to read it. Hector informed me that his mom was feeling a bit better and had returned to her second job, but that he recently had another asthma attack and had to go to a Chicago hospital for tests.

At the end of the letter was more concerning news. "My mom said they might make the oil refinery bigger so they can bring more really bad oil through the city. I don't completely understand all of it. But we are already planning to go to a protest soon."

I reached for my phone to text Uncle James. But I didn't have a phone. Punishment. Dang.

Then I remembered that we had an actual telephone! "Mom?"

She came into my room. "Yes?"

"Can I use the house phone to call Uncle James?"

"Sure."

Not surprisingly, Uncle James was aware of what Hector tried to explain in his letter. Several years earlier, the oil refinery in East City was expanded so it could receive tar sands oil from Canada, refine it, and ship it around the country. But tar sands oil is very thick and requires more of a machine-heavy process to be turned into fuel. It all adds up to a big mess for the environment.

Protests all over the U.S. and Canada in recent years had taken aim at tar sands and the underground pipelines that carry the oil. Now it was being reported that negotiations to dedicate even more space to refining tar sands and storing its toxic remnants, called petcoke, were taking place.

"As if that city hasn't been through enough already," Uncle James said.

"Is your work doing anything about it?" I asked.

"We will be. It sends a really bad message. The people of East City have felt like the government hasn't cared about them for years. This isn't gonna help that."

"And Hector said he was sick again and had to go to the hospital?"

"I hadn't heard that. I'll check in on him."

"Is there anything I can do to help?"

"I don't think so. But if there is, I'll let you know."

I didn't expect he'd encourage me to get involved. But I had every intention of doing so anyway. Somehow.

"**P**eople out here are really upset," Uncle James told me on the phone—still the house phone—a few days later. "They feel deceived."

I was worried about Hector. He already struggled with asthma, and I feared his health could get worse. During lunch that week at school, I vented my frustrations about the whole situation.

"East City has had problems with lead and air pollution and all kinds of stuff. And now there's this. I can't believe this is happening to them."

"Seriously." Rebecca nodded and then offered an analogy. "It's like, imagine your room is really messy, right? And you're trying to clean it up, but you keep making little messes too. And then you're making some progress one day when your little brother walks in the room and pees all over your floor."

We all stared at Rebecca with slightly amused smiles on our faces.

"Yeah, Becks," Ariana said, "it's exactly like that."

I felt the need to rescue the conversation from

absurdity. "I just wish we could do something. It's hard to sit out here and just let it happen."

"Mia, we live in Massachusetts," Ariana said. "And we're just kids. How are we gonna stop something about pollution in Indiana?"

"I don't know. I was kinda hoping you guys might have ideas."

"Well, if you can elect me president this afternoon, I'll make them stop."

Aliya wasn't so sure. "Maybe we can elect Christian or Conor. My aunt said it would take a miracle to get a woman president in the United States."

"Oh, that's so stupid," I said. "I love my dad and all, but if one of my parents was gonna be president, it better be my mom, or we're all doomed."

Naturally, Rebecca tried to stir up trouble. She looked at Conor and asked, "Would you vote for a woman?" With a grin, she then glanced at Ariana, who had developed a bit of a crush on Conor.

Conor then seemed to unknowingly play along with Rebecca's mischief. "If she's hot enough I would." His joke fell flat; we all shot him disapproving glares.

"Actually," Conor continued, "my dad left us when I was like three. My mom does everything for me and my brother. And her mom was a single mom, too. I honestly can't believe there's never been a woman president."

I noticed a sigh of relief with Ariana's smile. Then Aliya, who looked like she had been quietly thinking, changed the subject.

"Maybe the Climate Club can help," she said.

"Help Conor stop making bad jokes?" Rebecca quipped.

"No. With Mia's friend in Indiana."

"I wish we could," Christian said. "But what could we do? We can't go to any protests out there or anything."

Just then, Mr. Walker passed by our table and waved.

"Mr. Walker!" we shouted. We caught his attention so he stopped and grabbed the empty seat at our table.

"What's up? Everything okay?"

"Mia, tell him," Aliya said.

I explained what was happening in East City, that even more tar sands oil could become reality for the citizens there. People could already feel pollution in their lives, Uncle James had told me. They could see it in the oil slicks. They could smell it in the air. They could taste it in the water.

Then Aliya asked him, "Can the Climate Club do anything?"

"Christian is being a Debbie Downer and says we can't," Rebecca said. "Boys." She looked at Mr. Walker. "Am I right?"

We all laughed, but then Christian explained his thinking.

"I want to help. I just don't know what we can do from out here. We could have a fundraiser, but why will people out here give money for people in Indiana?"

"I don't know if they would," Mr. Walker said.

"See?" Rebecca chimed in, looking at her friends. "Boys!"

"Hold on, now." Mr. Walker knew Rebecca was joking, but he seemed determined to defend boys, something I certainly wouldn't want to try. "I didn't say we can't. But Christian's point is valid. People will rally to prevent pollution in their town or neighborhood, or even state. It's called NIMBY—Not In My Back Yard. But when it's other people, they usually don't care enough to actually do anything."

Then he added, "But it doesn't mean we can't try."

He looked at me.

"Something tells me you would want to at least try."

"I don't know how I can't," I said. "If people just let this go, won't it get even worse?"

"Of course it will. That's what keeps happening. It has throughout history. Things don't change until enough people speak up."

Feeling validated and inspired, I smiled slightly. "But what can we do?"

"I'll move up our next Climate Club meeting to this Wednesday. We'll talk about it. We'll come up with something we can try."

I looked at him to make sure he knew I meant it when I said, "Thanks, Mr. Walker."

"You're welcome."

Mr. Walker got up and left.

"I think I just discovered the secret to boys," Rebecca said. "Tell them how bad they are and then they'll surprise you!"

I left school feeling optimistic that day. When I got off the bus, I picked up Don's mail and read the note he had started the night of my visit.

Mia,
So great to see you today! Seeing your family
has given me a boost to work hard so I can get

home. You watch, I'll be running the Boston Marathon next year!

Thanks for getting my mail. My magazines are keeping me sane.

Take care. Please thank your family again for stopping by to see me.

Don

I wrote a quick response and tucked it into the box. I walked home smiling.

But the positive vibes soon went away. While I ate dinner that evening with Nate and Mom, Dad returned home from work.

"Honey," he said to Mom, "did you see that Kristin Cabral was next door at Don's?"

"No, I didn't." The concern on their faces was obvious.

This made me curious. "Who's that?"

Mom shook her head to stop Dad from answering, but luckily for me, the words were already coming out of his mouth.

"She's a real estate agent. Her son is in your class."

"Will Cabral?"

"I think so."

Then I realized why my parents reacted that way. Was Don's house being sold?

We opened the front door and saw Beth heading down Don's driveway. She saw us and walked over to say hi, and we greeted her out in our front yard.

"How are you all?" she asked.

"We're good," said Mom. "What about you?"

"Okay. You know, a lot going on. It was so great of you guys to go see my dad. It made his day."

"Is he okay?" I asked, sensing something was not right.

"Well, yeah, he's okay. It's just that he's eighty-six, almost eighty-seven. They're telling me that he might need a wheelchair for the rest of his life. At least to move around much."

Dad broached the subject that had prompted us to go outside in the first place. "I guess that's why Kristin Cabral was over?"

"Oh, yeah." Beth seemed caught off guard. She looked at Mom and said with an awkward smile, "I thought you were the reporter in the family."

"My husband scooped me on this one."

"Well, we have not decided that we're selling his house. And he has no idea that I met with a Realtor, so I'm hoping we can keep that between us."

"Of course," Mom said.

"We just want to explore our options," Beth continued, "get a feel for the housing market out here. This house has two floors and a basement. That's a lot of stairs. And it's an hour from me. If he needs a lot of help, this house, and its location, is not ideal."

What she said made total sense to all of us, yet we returned to the dinner table with a sense of sadness. I imagined Don living in a nursing home and being pushed around in a wheelchair, which happened to my great-grandmother.

But Great Memere, who had died when I was in third grade, had been ninety-three, frail, and nearly deaf. She had forgotten who Nate and I were by the last year of her life.

Don was different. Until Reggie, Don still did yard work, shoveled snow off his driveway—at least until Dad and Nate showed up with shovels and insisted he take a break—and still remembered everything.

It seemed so unfair that one accident, one storm, caused by a crazy climate sent into a spiral by us humans, would leave him in a wheelchair in a nursing home.

That night, with Don still on my mind, I sat on the couch next to my mom.

"Mom, is there anything we'd be able to do to help Don stay here? Like go over there and help him a few times a day? Get his groceries? Take care of his house?"

Mom smiled.

"Unfortunately, that would be beyond us," she said. "We have enough trouble keeping up with our own busy lives. And helping an old man in a wheelchair is not something that just anyone can do. People get special training for that. What if we caused an accident or something?"

Unfortunately, I knew Mom was right.

"Plus," she continued, "Don would never be okay with that. He'd feel too much like a burden. Why do you think he almost never asks us for anything? He doesn't want to impose. Your dad has told him a thousand times that we could cut his lawn, shovel his driveway, help him spread mulch in his garden, pick up his groceries. Never. When he goes away for a few days, he asks us to get his mail and call one of his children if a tree falls on his house. That's it."

We both laughed. Then, accepting Mom's common-sense explanation, I went to brush my teeth and get ready for bed.

As I tried to fall asleep that night, I thought there was a very real chance that the day of Hurricane Reggie would prove to be Don's last in his house. All I could do was hope he made more progress than the doctors expected and returned to his old self—or at least close to it.

Chapter

"Hey Mia, have you gotten any of those secret admirer notes lately?" Rebecca asked me at our lockers after school one day as we filled our backpacks with books and binders before heading to our Climate Club meeting.

"No."

"So that *must* mean it was Matt O'Connor, right?"

"Why?"

"Because, the notes stopped after you yelled at him for the whole water bottle thing. It makes total sense."

I shrugged. "Maybe." That would have been just fine with me.

As we entered the classroom, Mr. Walker encouraged us to quickly take a seat. He then projected a video on his whiteboard, and we all stared at it, mouths agape, disbelief etched on our faces.

It was the beginning of December, and Mr. Walker opened the meeting by showing us a news clip of wildfires burning in California that very day.

On the screen were massive fires—the entire

whiteboard enveloped in orange. Firefighters made feeble attempts to extinguish them with hoses. The news reporter said, "These fires are becoming more intense now, scientists say, because of the unpredictability caused by climate change."

When the video ended, Mr. Walker calmly asked a question: "How does this make you feel?"

Our hands went up and answers came flying back.

"Scared."

"Shocked."

"Like I was watching a sci-fi movie."

"Worried."

"Sad."

Christian's answer also captured my emotion: "Angry."

"Why?" Mr. Walker asked.

"Because they said climate change is making this worse," he said. "*We're* making this worse."

"And this is why I called this meeting on short notice," Mr. Walker said. "We are contributing to these climate problems every day. When we drive cars and burn oil in Plymouth, we are adding to climate disruptions across the globe. It's just the reality."

He paused and looked at me.

"Do you want to tell everyone about your friend?"

"Okay."

I stood up. I was pretty nervous, to the point that I could feel my heart beating and my hands sweating. I wondered how the other kids would respond. East City was a thousand miles away. Why would they care? It would be easy to rally them if the problem was in Plymouth, or Carver, or even Boston. But East City, Indiana?

Mr. Walker encouraged me. "Just tell them what you told me at lunch the other day."

I took a deep breath.

"When I went to Chicago after Reggie, I made a friend," I began. "His name is Hector, and he lives in East City, Indiana. I mentioned him before in one of our meetings. He has kind of a hard life compared to us, and a lot of it is because of the pollution there. He grew up around it all. The government has had to clean a bunch of the soil because it's so contaminated."

I briefly paused and scanned the room. It seemed that most of them were interested. I continued.

"Well, there's an oil refinery in the city. All kinds of pollution goes into the air. And now they're making plans to bring in more of this really bad oil called tar sands. It comes from Canada and then gets shipped around the country."

I looked at Mr. Walker's calming smile, which helped me to relax a little more. Then I thought about Hector.

"Hector has had two asthma attacks before. I'm worried about him. But it's not just him. I've seen where he lives. It's not like it is here. I can't imagine living there. And now it's gonna get even more polluted there. It's just not fair."

Mr. Walker interjected, making sure that everyone could make a connection between East City and Plymouth: "And as far away as East City may seem, pollution anywhere impacts people all over the world. As Martin Luther King once wrote, 'Injustice anywhere is a threat to justice everywhere.'"

Mrs. Young chimed in. "Absolutely. It certainly affects the people of East City more than us. But it's a global problem. Like we talked about in the first meeting, our pollution, our fossil fuels, they are a problem for Africa, Asia, in some ways more than they even are for us."

"How can we fix the climate if we just use more and more oil?" Christian asked rhetorically.

"Yeah," I said. "I want to help Hector, but it's more than that. When will this end?"

"Some of you know that I am from Chicago," Mr. Walker said. "I certainly know a bit about East City, but I did a little research the other night. Lead poisoning has been a devastating problem for East City. Lead causes so many problems, but it really messes with the brains of children. They have had to tear down a housing complex and make all the residents leave because of the lead in the soil."

My eyes opened very wide. "Hector used to live there!" I blurted out before realizing that I had kind of interrupted him. "Sorry, Mr. Walker."

"No, it's okay." He continued. "So as Mia mentioned, there's an oil refinery in part of the city, where they turn crude oil into all sorts of fuel for cars, planes, to heat homes. When they refine the tar sands, it creates this leftover stuff called petroleum coke, or petcoke, which is some kind of dusty oil byproduct that is blowing through the East City neighborhoods. Petcoke is mostly used in other parts of the world where they aren't as strict about pollution. Yet it's created and stored in East City."

The room was quiet initially. My friends and I looked around, wondering how the group would react. Finally, a sixth-grade boy named Jeff asked, "What can we do? We're not in Indiana."

That was my fear. "I don't know," I said. "I was hoping we could come up with some ideas."

"Let me ask this," Mrs. Young said. "Is this something you would want to get involved in?"

A few silent nods gradually swelled into a room full of them, accompanied by several voices. "Yeah." "Definitely."

"Sounds like a yes to me," Mr. Walker said, smiling at me. "But we need to discuss what we can do."

Ideas were tossed about. Carwash. Bake sale. Collect change at the cafeteria. Mr. Walker and Mrs. Young said they liked the ideas, but they encouraged us to think bigger.

"A little pocket change from Massachusetts won't do much," Mr. Walker said. "Not that it would hurt. But people around here aren't going to empty their pockets for a pollution problem in Indiana. It's just the reality."

Christian's hand went up. "What if we started a social media account? When certain hashtags start trending, it can get a lot of attention." He looked at me, and his embarrassed smile seemed to say, "Remember the hashtag that made us skip school?"

"I love that idea!" Mrs. Young said. "Principal Lewis is always encouraging us to have a social media presence. We can set up Instagram and Twitter accounts that directly involve you guys."

Then came a voice from the back corner of the room.

"What if we held a protest in front of the school and invited local TV stations?" the voice said. It was a familiar voice to me. I whipped my head around, peered between a few faces, and spotted Matt O'Connor.

Matt O'Connor? At the Climate Club?

I was too stunned to reply, but Mr. Walker was impressed.

"Now *that* could drum up support! Good thinking! Of course, I'd have to get the okay from Principal Lewis. She might not like that—getting a principal to agree to let thirty-some students miss an hour of school to protest for something in another state—"

He stopped and seemed to be thinking about something. That was good, because I needed a minute to process the shock of seeing Matt O'Connor at a Climate Club meeting. And producing a good idea!

Then Mr. Walker picked up the phone from his desk and pressed a few numbers.

"Hi Mrs. Lewis," he said. "Do you happen to have a few minutes free right now? We'd like to pitch something to you. Okay great, see you in a minute."

He turned to the class.

"She's coming here now." He broke out in a mischievous grin. "She might have a harder time saying no to a room full of students than just to Mrs. Young and me." I loved his thinking.

I was fidgety with nervous energy as I awaited the principal's arrival, twirling a pencil in my hand and turning to chat with my friends. Mr. Walker asked me if I'd explain the background, and of course I agreed. When Principal Lewis walked in the door, she smiled at us and then looked at the teachers.

"What's going on? What's this pitch all about?"

"Well," Mr. Walker said. "I'll let Mia give you the details first."

Despite almost shaking with nerves initially, I told our principal about Hector and East City and lead and petcoke. The whole story.

"And as Mr. Walker said, pollution anywhere affects people everywhere," I concluded.

"So," Mr. Walker said, "We have an idea. Matt, would you explain?"

He started to speak when Principal Lewis smiled and interrupted him.

"Stand up, Mr. O'Connor, I can't even see you way back there!"

He stood. "We want to have a protest. In front of the school. And call TV news and newspapers to come to it. We think people would notice that."

Mrs. Young added her voice to the pitch. "Imagine what it could do, the impact it might have, if kids in Massachusetts care so much about the environment that they're protesting pollution and speaking up for other kids a thousand miles away."

Principal Lewis thought about it for half a minute or so.

"First of all, I love your compassion, your dedication to such an important cause. I've seen your posters, talked to your two teachers here, and I can tell that you all are taking this very seriously. And someone needs to. I applaud you for that."

Then I braced myself for the next word to be "But" or "However."

"As for a protest, I think that could be very powerful. I'm going to tentatively say yes…"

She said yes? We looked at each other with smiles that started small but quickly grew. But we suppressed our voices to be sure not to upset Principal Lewis.

"I do have a few conditions," she continued. "All of the details will need to be worked out with me first by your teachers, and you must—absolutely *must*—stick to the plan and be on your best behavior. This will not be unruly. You'll represent our school and our town the right way."

We all nodded in agreement.

"And I will find the right time for this to take place so that you miss as little time on learning as possible."

She looked at all of our excited faces.

"Sound fair?"

"Yes, Principal Lewis," we said in something close to unison.

"Okay then. I'll be in touch with Mr. Walker and Mrs. Young, and they'll give you all the details. Now, it's just about time for the late bus, so I'll leave you to wrap things up. Have a great rest of your day!"

We all thanked her, and Mr. Walker instructed us to get our stuff. "Great job, everyone," he said. He looked at me and gave me a thumb's up.

After I thanked my friends for their help, I rushed over to Matt O'Connor, who was leaving the room.

"Hey Matt," I called.

"Oh, hey." He seemed surprised I was chasing him down.

"Thanks for coming to the meeting today. And that was a great idea you had."

"Thanks."

I grinned. "Can I ask you something?"

"Sure."

"What made you decide to join? You've kind of been hostile to me about this stuff before."

"I don't know," he said. "I had a lunch detention with Mrs. Young last week. I saw something about the Climate Club on her board, and I knew you were in it. So I asked her about it. Then I searched up some things when I got home. I realized I was kind of being an idiot, that this stuff is pretty important."

The thought behind his answer surprised me. "Oh. Well, I'm glad you came."

"Me too." He saw several other students heading down the hall. "I gotta get going. Late bus."

"Okay, see ya later."

"See ya."

I turned around and saw my friends approaching.

"Everything okay?" asked Christian.

"Yeah. I just wanted to know why he came. He's been kind of a jerk to me about it before."

"What did he say?" Ariana asked.

"I guess Mrs. Young talked to him about it during a detention or something."

Rebecca wasn't buying it. "Please, he's here for you. We all know it."

Christian seemed perplexed. "We all know what?"

"Oh, he's had a crush on Mia for a while," Rebecca said. "But Mia finds him arrogant and annoying. And she's kind of right."

The look of relief on Christian's face made me happy in a weird, hard-to-explain sort of way.

Rebecca then capitalized on the chance to tease Christian a little. "Maybe she finds him slightly less annoying after today, though, right Mia?"

"Only slightly," I said, laughing to myself.

Part

3

East
City

Chapter

"How about this?" Rebecca said excitedly. "Ready? Here it is: 'Join the fight against climate change, or we will put a curse on you. So your choices are help or get cursed. Make the right choice. #AvoidTheCurse #Don'tBeSelfishIdiots.'

"So? Whaddya think?"

We all looked at each other and at her, not sure whether to laugh or to tell her she was nuts.

"The sentiment is okay," Mr. Walker finally said in as nice a way as possible. "But perhaps it's a little too harsh. You know, to call them selfish idiots."

"No," Rebecca said with a smile, "I'm telling them how to *not* be selfish idiots. I'm being helpful!"

We had a good laugh, but we were actually working on serious stuff. After our meeting about East City, the Climate Club developed somewhat of a social media presence, which was fun for me since my parents didn't allow me to have my own social media accounts. And using my mom's Twitter to find a protest I could sneak off to wasn't going to convince them to change their rule anytime soon.

To Rebecca's dismay, we didn't threaten anyone with curses (I will say that if Mr. Walker had somehow been okay with her tweet, I wouldn't have tried to stop it!). Instead, since we had noticed the use of the hashtag #letECbreathe, we decided to adopt it and run with it. We added #PlymouthSupportsEC. We took several photos of each other, in many cases wearing surgical masks to illustrate the difficulty breathing polluted air. In each of these, whoever was in the picture held up a sign. Something like:

> The kids of East City deserve to breathe clean air
>
> Pollution anywhere hurts all of us everywhere
>
> Clean our planet. Including East City

Learning about East City inspired us even more. Residents there had fought hard for their rights to live and raise children in a cleaner city. Most of East City was industrial, with an oil refinery and steel mills and energy companies. We learned that oil had been a part of East City since the late 1800s. We could not relate to this. Plymouth had a nuclear power plant that my mom had mentioned before—I guess it made her a little nervous—but it wasn't actively polluting our air.

Mr. Walker also submitted some blurbs to read over the morning announcements, designed to make the entire student body aware of the cause we had adopted.

The date of the protest had been finalized for a Wednesday in mid-December. Principal Lewis, who had worked in Plymouth for her entire career and seemed to know everyone, told me before school one morning that she had made a few phone calls to reporters and was optimistic that some would show up—possibly even a TV station.

I kept Uncle James updated about the club's effort, which impressed him, though I didn't exactly think he expected a group of middle schoolers in Massachusetts to make a serious impact.

Still, I wrote letters to Hector and said the Climate Club was working hard, that my teacher, a Chicago native, cared about the issue, and that we would not give up. It made me feel better to write the words, because I had doubts.

I mean, will this really accomplish anything?

Then I'd catch myself wavering and snap out of it.

It can't hurt to try.

Meanwhile, as winter approached, my basketball team began practicing for the season. This gave me a very full plate. I was working as hard as ever on the Climate Club, and the amount of homework was annoyingly on the rise as the second term began. It was seriously getting in the way of what I actually wanted to do.

One evening the week before our protest, Mom came to my room while I was reading and texting on my phone, which I had recently—finally—gotten back.

"Have you finished your homework yet?" she asked.

I barely looked up from my phone. "Yeah. I finished when I got home from school, like usual."

"Your English homework, too?"

"I didn't have any."

She continued to look at me but didn't speak. I began to feel like there was an interrogation going on. I put down my phone.

"Why do you ask?"

"Well, I got an email from your English teacher today."

I felt a pit in my stomach. I was pretty sure what the email was about, but I didn't think the teacher would actually tell my mom.

"She says you missed a homework assignment last week," Mom said, "and that today, you only got two out of ten right on a quiz from last night's reading. What's going on?"

"I'm sorry," I said half-heartedly.

"Well that's good, but that doesn't answer my question."

I shrugged. "I don't like the book we're reading."

"I don't like going to the grocery store after working eight hours," Mom responded. "But we have responsibilities. And it's unlike you to not do your homework."

"I know," I said, trying not to feel as guilty as she wanted me to. "I usually do my English reading in here after dinner, but sometimes when I come in here to read, I get distracted."

"By your phone?"

"No. Well, kind of. Not texting or anything. But sometimes I start reading articles about the climate instead of my English book."

Mom's reaction didn't show anger, surprise, or anything. She was totally calm. I hated when she did that.

"Okay, well I believe you have two options. You can either do your English homework in the kitchen before dinner, like your other subjects. Or I can keep all electronics out of your room, including your phone, on school nights."

I didn't love either option.

"Isn't it better if I'm reading about something really important than just a random book about people that some author made up?" I asked.

Mom sighed. "I understand where you're coming from. But you know that's not how it works. Many times I get assigned a story that doesn't interest me. I'd rather write about something else. But I have a job to do. I have to listen to my boss. As a student, your job is to listen to your teachers."

I gave it some thought. Before I responded, Mom offered a suggestion.

"Why don't you just get it done before dinner, and then you'll have the rest of the night to focus on things that interest you."

I begrudgingly agreed.

The next day, I stuck to that plan; I worked on my assigned English reading while Mom prepared dinner. While reading, I stumbled upon an unfamiliar concept: feedback loop. A character in the book discussed the feedback loop of her coffee addiction—she'd drink coffee to stay awake, and that coffee would make it harder for her to sleep the next night. Therefore, she'd wake up tired and need even more coffee.

I opened the computer and searched for feedback loops to help myself understand better. But in my search, I found several interesting and disturbing feedback loops related to climate change.

For example, the hotter the planet gets, the more fuel will be burned to power air conditioning. That fuel goes back into the air as emissions, making the climate even hotter, leading to more air conditioning, and again, more emissions. Feedback loop.

I read another. Like a giant mirror, ice in the arctic reflects the sun back off of the earth to keep the planet cooler. As the planet warms, the ice melts. Less ice means less heat from the sun is reflected away, increasing the temperature on Earth even more. Feedback loop.

I kind of freaked out. *How will this ever be stopped?* I called Mom over and showed it to her.

"Didn't we just talk about staying focused on your English?"

"Yeah, I am." I explained the connection to her. Then I showed her the climate feedback loops.

Mom nodded and said, "It makes sense, unfortunately." Then she looked at me, seeing that I was clearly irritated by this discovery. "You're making yourself crazy by reading this stuff so much."

"I can't help it, Mom." I transitioned back to feedback loops. "The worse it gets, the faster things will heat up. Did you see the fires in California?"

I stared down at the keyboard. "I'd like to know that there's some plan out there somewhere. That people are working on this and everyone else will start listening to them."

I think it was that night that Mom truly realized how important climate change was to me, how much it bothered me, that it was not a phase I would simply pass through. After dinner, she ordered a climate change book for her e-reader.

It looked like she was prepared to join me, and Uncle James, and my school friends, and Hector, in the cause.

The next morning at school, something happened that hadn't in several weeks.

There was a new note in my locker. It read:

Your smile makes me smile. Your laugh makes me laugh.

"Becks!" I whisper-shouted while purposefully motioning to Rebecca. "Get over here!"

I showed her the new note.

"Oh, it's gotta be Matt O'Connor!" Rebecca said.

"How do you figure?"

"Come on! You don't see it? There was no note for weeks after you almost ripped his head off about the water bottle."

I laughed and interrupted her. "Every time you tell that story, I sound meaner!"

Rebecca continued. "Anyway, now that he came to that meeting and you talked to him, suddenly there's another letter?"

"Well, that meeting was over a week ago."

"Okay, so who else could it be?"

"I have no idea."

"Aren't you dying to know?" Rebecca asked.

I stared down at the note. "Yeah, pretty much."

Chapter

The morning of the protest, I woke up unusually early. I made sure to wear nice leggings and a cute sweater dress and pull my hair into a tight ponytail. If I was going to be on TV that day, I wasn't going to look like a slob.

I sat alone at the kitchen table just before six o'clock when my phone buzzed. It was Christian.

"You ready for this?" he texted.

"Yeah. You?"

"Yeah. Kinda excited."

"Me too."

"See ya soon."

I sent back a thumbs-up emoji and returned to my English muffin and orange juice. But I felt antsy. I was ready to get on with it, but the next hour seemed to last three. I watched some YouTube videos to distract myself.

As I finally stood up to leave for the bus, I received another text. It was Uncle James. The text was a picture of him, Hector, and Tracey, all smiling, with the following message: "Saw these guys last night at a community meeting to discuss the pollution. We all wish you luck today!"

The plan called for the students in the Climate Club to meet Mr. Walker and Mrs. Young in the lobby after lunch. A daily twenty-five-minute block used for makeup work and free-choice reading followed lunch, so less class time would be sacrificed for the protest. The teachers would hold onto our signs and masks and deliver them to us when lunch ended. Then we would all sit on the school's front lawn, holding the signs and wearing the masks, visible to all passersby. Many in the community already knew of the protest thanks to social media and word of mouth.

We knew that we had to be on our best behavior. No talking. Just sitting. That would more powerfully make our point. It was a serious issue, and we needed to project that seriousness.

I actually no longer felt nervous as we walked out the front door of the school toward our designated spot. In the past, I might have fretted about how others would view my actions. Would they think I was taking it too seriously? Just trying to get attention?

On this day, none of that entered my mind. I believed so much in what we were doing.

Halfway from the school's main door to our protest location, I felt a nudge from Rebecca. I looked at my best friend, who motioned with her head toward one of the side parking lots.

I glanced in that direction and immediately spotted a van with a logo from a Boston TV station. Leaning on the van was a man and a large camera, and next to him, another man, this one dressed in a blue coat and holding a microphone. On his coat and microphone was that same logo from the van.

Not far from them stood a woman about my mom's age, holding a thin notebook with the spiral binding on the top. I recognized those as reporter's notebooks, which I had seen around my own house for much of my life.

We arrived at our spot on the school's front lawn, and there Mr. Walker, Mrs. Young, and the students of the Climate Club sat in complete silence, masks covering our mouths and noses, signs in hand, for sixty minutes. Some drivers slowed down to look, and others beeped their horns and waved in support. Most did neither.

My friends and I exchanged glances on a few occasions. We could smile under our masks, and no one could really tell. I noticed, out of the corner of my eye, Matt O'Connor, whose idea we had put into action and who had seemingly completed a 180-degree turn on the issue of climate change. I also noticed Mrs. Young and thought that, while she was protesting in support of East City, she was really there for children all over the globe, including her baby daughter, whose future—like the rest of ours—would be impacted by how the world deals with the climate.

Then Mr. Walker rose. The time was up.

"Single-file line, please," he said calmly. He didn't have to shout. His was the only voice.

Mrs. Young began to lead us back inside, but Mr. Walker approached me and motioned for me to walk with him in a different direction.

"I should have asked you this before, but I didn't know for sure that reporters would be here," he said. "Would you mind talking to them about this?"

"Okay," I said with some apprehension; I had never spoken to a reporter about anything, let alone with a giant camera pointed at me.

"Great," Mr. Walker said. "Who else do you think would be good for them to talk to?"

I pondered the question for a few seconds. "Maybe Christian and Aliya?"

"You don't think Aliya would be too shy?"

"I don't know. But she knows a lot about it, and she's super smart."

"Okay." Mr. Walker then took a few long strides to catch up with the line, and he quickly returned with Christian and Aliya. Christian looked more confident about the prospect of an interview than Aliya, but she agreed to it.

Mr. Walker spoke to the TV station first while the newspaper reporter interviewed the students. She identified herself as Elaine from the *South Shore Gazette*.

"Can you guys tell me how this all got started?"

Aliya and Christian looked at me, expecting that I'd go first.

"My friend lives in East City," I said. "He has asthma and has been affected by the pollution there. He's been protesting this plan to bring more tar sands oil to the city because it's going to lead to even more pollution. So we wanted to do something to show support."

"It's interesting that you're protesting pollution in Indiana," Elaine said. "Have you found that people support you?"

Then Aliya, to my pleasant surprise, jumped right in. "Some people do. Nobody has said anything bad about it to us. I guess a lot of people don't care too much about what we're doing, and they haven't cared all along since we started the Climate Club after the hurricane."

"Is that why you started the Climate Club?" Elaine asked. "Because of how bad Reggie was?"

"Yeah," I said. "That's when I started to learn about climate change, and how it's causing bad storms and fires and other problems. But Christian knew more about it before."

"Oh?"

"Sort of," Christian said. "I have family in Brazil, and I've heard so much about the Amazon getting burned down. My parents had told me a lot of stuff. That's what got me into the club."

"So what will you do next?"

"We don't know yet," Aliya said. "Whatever we can do to help. We want to help. Even if it's just posting on social media."

"And why do you all care so much about climate change?"

"It's our future," Christian and I said in unison, prompting us to smile at each other. Then I added, "I just don't know how someone could possibly not care about it."

Elaine thanked us and made sure to get the spelling of our names exactly correct. When I spelled my last name, Elaine stopped writing. "Is your mom Sovannary?"

"Yeah."

"No way! I worked with her for a little while in Taunton before she took time off. I see her sometimes when we cover the same things. She's great! Tell her I said hi!"

"Okay, I will."

Mr. Walker had just finished his TV interview and came to switch places with me. He told Christian and Aliya that only one student would speak to the TV reporter, which seemed to bring relief to Aliya and mild disappointment to Christian.

The questions were similar, but the wording of one in particular led me to go on what I guess I could call a little rant.

"Why should people of Massachusetts care about pollution in East City, Indiana?"

"Because it's all the same air and the same planet," I said, just getting started. "The earth isn't only getting warmer in the areas where people pollute a lot. When we use too much coal and oil, anyone in the world could suffer. It's not fair. And my friend in East City shouldn't have to breathe in dirty air because some company doesn't care about him. Shouldn't we all care about him? And the people in other places where there's so much pollution? It's not just their problem. It's everyone's."

The reporter shook my hand. I then turned toward the school, somewhat stunned by my own answer to that last question. *Where did that come from?* I wondered. When I looked up, I noticed Principal Lewis a few feet away.

"Wow, Mia," she said, laughing. "You gave me chills. This might be your calling."

As I walked in the building and down the hall to math class, I thought about Elaine's question: What's next? I wasn't thinking so much about what the Climate Club would do; rather, would there be any response from others? Would anyone even notice? Or would our protest take the same route as so many others, seemingly off a cliff and into the abyss, rarely to be thought about again.

Chapter

I was still running on adrenaline when I hopped off the bottom step of the school bus that afternoon. I briskly walked to Don's mailbox, grabbed the mail, and took it into the house. I smiled when I saw a note from Don, a simple, straightforward note that contained one particularly encouraging line: "I'm working really hard on my physical therapy, and the nurses say I'm doing great."

Feeling hopeful, and with my mind still racing from the day's events, I penned a longer note to Don. I described the protest and explained my commitment to the cause of fighting climate change, providing some of the back story. Based on the book I had seen beside his bed, I figured he'd understand.

I also wrote, "I saw the newspaper article on your wall. My dad says you protested for rights for Black people when you were younger. I'd love to talk to you about that someday. Maybe you would have some advice for me."

I left the note in the cardboard box of mail and

walked across the lawn toward my own house when I saw Mom's car in the driveway. This gave me an uncomfortable feeling in my stomach because Mom was almost never home before four o'clock. There were days when she would work really late, like if she had to cover a town meeting or some other nighttime event. But this? Very unexpected.

I walked through the door with some trepidation. I so badly wanted to tell Mom all about the protest, the TV interview, the reporter who used to work at the *Herald*. But I was enveloped by a sense of concern.

"Hey Mom," I said.

"Hey! How's it going? I want to hear all about your big day. I've been dying for you to get home!"

"Okay. But why are you home? Is everything all right?"

"Yeah, everything's fine."

"How come you're home this early?"

"Oh, just had a different kind of day today. I'll tell you about it when Nate gets home."

I felt no less concerned, but Mom pressed on.

"So go ahead, tell me about the protest. Did it all go okay?"

"Yeah," I said, my enthusiasm sliced to half of what it had been just a few minutes earlier. "It was weird sitting silently for so long like that, but everyone did it. It seemed to go well. I met someone who knows you. Elaine something. She works for a newspaper."

"Elaine McDermott? *South Shore Gazette*?"

"Yeah, that's the one."

"Wow! We used to work together. I always liked Elaine. Wish we had worked together longer. So did she interview you or something?"

"Yeah. And I think I'm gonna be on TV!"

"What?" Mom's face really brightened. "Really?"

"I know! A guy from Channel 4 asked me questions. I talked into his microphone. It was so weird."

"This is amazing! We need to make sure we watch the news tonight." Mom turned on the TV. "I'll set the DVR now, just in case. We can't take any chances."

Then she looked at me. Like, really looked at me. "I'm so proud of you," she said. "You've really dedicated yourself to this."

I thought I was about to get choked up, but just then, Nate burst through the door and looked directly at me.

"Hey, I heard you're gonna be on TV."

"Maybe. How do you know that?"

"Jason told me."

Jason was one of Nate's lacrosse friends. His sister was also in seventh grade, though not in the Climate Club, and I didn't know her that well.

"Geez, word spreads fast, apparently."

"Did you give me a shout out?" he asked. I rolled my eyes at him, though a slight smile poked its way through.

"Why are you home, Mom?" Nate asked.

Oh yeah. That abruptly ended my brief respite from worry.

Mom sighed. "Sit down. I want to talk to both of you at the same time about this."

"That's not a great way to start a conversation," Nate said, echoing my sentiments.

"I can't say that this is unexpected," she began. "Newspapers around the country, especially small local papers, have been struggling for years now. I was lucky when I got hired back seven years ago—they needed a reporter, and they knew me from when I worked there before. But today, they told us that they had to cut a bunch of jobs, including some reporters and copy editors. Mine was one of those jobs."

I gasped and put my hand over my mouth. Nate looked angry. Mom, as usual, stayed remarkably composed.

"Are we gonna be okay?" I asked. "Are *you* okay?"

"We'll be fine. They're giving me a couple of weeks' pay, and I'll go on unemployment until I can find a job. I don't want you to worry about that. Your father has a good job." She paused. "We'll take it one day at a time. That's all we can do."

"Will you look for another newspaper job?" Nate asked.

"Honestly, I haven't even thought that far ahead yet. Probably not, since there are so few of those jobs. We'll see."

I had felt on the verge of tears as the news was delivered, but Mom's calm demeanor managed to assuage me for the moment.

"So what do you guys want for dinner tonight?" Mom asked. "I have more time to cook something than usual."

"You pick, Mom," I said.

Nate agreed. "Yeah. Whatever you want. Surprise us."

"Wow! Okay, sounds good to me."

I looked at Mom again, trying to see if she was more bothered by this than she was letting on. "Is there anything I can do to help?" I asked.

"With dinner?"

"Yeah. Or anything else."

"You can do a great job on your homework. And keep being you." Then she smiled. "Other than the whole skipping school and going to Boston thing."

I grabbed my backpack and took out my homework. I worked on it in the kitchen that afternoon so that I could be closer to Mom.

That night, we watched the news before dinner—I was happy that Dad made it home in time. The images on the TV included all of our solemn faces, all wearing masks that covered our noses and mouths. The camera locked in on some signs.

We stand with East City #letECbreathe
Pollution anywhere hurts all of us everywhere

Mr. Walker and Principal Lewis were both interviewed, and a few minutes into the segment, I had only seen myself as a tiny face in the crowd.

Then suddenly, there I was. It was one of the weirdest moments of my life, seeing my face and the top half of the microphone, which was angled in my direction. My name briefly flashed on the bottom. I felt a little embarrassed, but mostly proud. Thankfully, it was my best answer that appeared. The whole thing!

"It's not just their problem. It's everyone's." That's how the segment ended before the anchors in the studio went on to their next topic.

My entire family looked at me, like they were waiting for me to say something, or at least show some emotion. I looked back at them and fought unsuccessfully to suppress a smile.

Nate's eyes opened really wide. "Dude, you were amazing!"

"I'm floored right now," Dad followed. "Absolutely floored. Not that I'd expect anything less, but still!"

Mom, who had been sitting next to me the whole time, leaned over and hugged me, which felt even better than her normal hugs.

"This girl's gonna do big things in the world," she said. "Don't get in her way!"

Even before those words had been spoken, my phone was buzzing so much that it appeared to be dancing on the coffee table.

"Go ahead," Dad said, "we know you want to check it."

So I did.

From Ariana: "You were so awesome!"

Christian: "You're a star!"

Then Rebecca: "Hey, remember that it was my idea to start the Climate Club." A winking emoji followed.

I responded: "I'll never forget that. Ur the best."

"Yes. Yes I am," Rebecca replied. "And great job. You were perfect."

"Thanks."

I spent some time that night texting with my friends, fending off good-natured ribbing from Nate, and trying to unwind from such a whirlwind day.

At one point, around 9:15, I headed down the stairs toward the kitchen for a drink of water when I heard what sounded like laughing coming from my parents' room, which was the only downstairs bedroom. I approached the door, eager to join in whatever was making them happy.

But before I could grab the doorknob, I realized that it was not laughter that I was hearing. Mom was crying. Dad was doing his best to console her.

I desperately wanted to open the door. The urge to comfort and help my mom was almost overwhelming, but I resisted. They were behind a closed door for a reason, I thought. Mom didn't want Nate and me to see how upset she really was about losing her job.

I struggled to fall asleep that night. My thoughts bounced back and forth like a rally in a tennis match. One minute it was the protest and the TV news; the next, it was Mom's job and how it might impact us all. Back and forth. Toss and turn.

But Mom continued to put on a brave face, so much so that I quickly adjusted to the new normal of seeing her before and after school most days. It was really nice, actually.

Often I would see her reading her climate change book on the e-reader, and we'd discuss some of the details. Together we were learning more about climate change, as well as possible ways to address it.

Meanwhile, two days after the protest and the airing of the news segment, I was alerted to an interesting development.

Soon after Aliya, Rebecca, and I started our walk down to the cafeteria for lunch that day, we heard Mr. Walker's voice from his classroom.

"Hey girls!" he said with urgency. "Come here! Come here! You gotta see this!"

We all but sprinted to his desk, eager to see what had him so excited. He tilted his computer screen toward us, showing us a Twitter post with a picture of the Channel 4 anchor who had interviewed Mr. Walker and me. A triangle in the center indicated it was a video clip.

"What's the video?" Rebecca asked.

Mr. Walker pointed to the top of the screen. "Look at this. This is Channel 4's Twitter feed. They posted the story on us. Look how many retweets and comments!"

He pointed to the retweet symbol. The number next to it was 157! We couldn't believe it! Our usual tweets from the Climate Club's account were lucky to get a handful of retweets, and they were either from our parents or school administrators. Aliya clutched my arm in excitement.

"And this was just posted yesterday," Mr. Walker added. "There are a lot of comments, and they're all so supportive."

This was *exactly* what I hoped would happen, that people would take an interest. I didn't want all of our effort to feel like it had been wasted.

I read one comment on the screen: "I'm from East City. Been dealing with pollution my whole life. Amazed these kids out there are doing this. So touched."

Then Mr. Walker scrolled down to another: "Love that girl! The world needs more kids like her!"

"Mia, you're famous!" Rebecca blurted out.

Was there actually a chance our voices were being heard? Enough to make a difference? I felt something that had eluded me since I developed an interest in climate change: optimism.

In the coming days, the spread of our voices only accelerated. My phone rang a few nights later, and Uncle James was on the other end of a FaceTime.

"Mimi, why didn't you tell me that you're a celebrity now?" he joked. "No, but seriously, this is kind of a big deal. I retweeted that story and sent the link to a lot of people. The fact that a school in Massachusetts is speaking up like you guys are is really making a difference."

With some sense of pride, I said, "That's great, Uncle James!"

"I'm with some people who want to say hi," he added. He turned his phone to one side, and Hector and Tracey appeared on my screen, smiling and waving frantically.

"Hey Mia," they said.

"Hey guys!"

"It's so great to see you!" said Tracey.

"You guys too!"

Hector poked his head into the picture. "Thanks for what you're doing for us."

"Really," Tracey said. "It means so much to us. You have no idea."

I was somewhat uncomfortable with the praise. After all, Hector and Tracey attended protests and rallies regularly, surrounded by dozens, even hundreds of their fellow East City residents, a commitment that appeared to go virtually unnoticed. And they were the ones living with the polluted air and contaminated soil. But if the Climate Club had succeeded in putting East City into the minds of more people, then I'd get over my discomfort.

"How are you feeling, Hector?" I asked.

"Pretty good. They changed my inhaler. I just have to make sure I always have it with me."

Tracey gave him a firm but loving look. "Yes, you do!"

Uncle James's face reappeared on the screen. "We need to go. A member of the City Council is giving a talk about this issue inside in a few minutes. We need to get our seats."

"Okay," I said. "Good luck. Bye guys!"

"Bye Mia!" they said in unison.

"Japan!"

"Nope. Anyone else?"

"North Korea."

"Not quite. Other guesses?"

In my social studies class one morning, Mr. Walker had asked us to identify a country on the map in Southeast Asia. I was examining it very closely. I knew where Cambodia was because my mom and Nana had shown me before. The mystery country was long and skinny and bordered Cambodia.

Feeling limited confidence, I took a guess. "Thailand?"

"No, Mia, but you're very close," Mr. Walker said. "It's actually Vietnam."

We let out a collective groan. We obviously didn't know where Vietnam was, but we had certainly heard of it.

"What comes to mind when you think of Vietnam?" Mr. Walker asked them.

Many students said the Vietnam War, though a girl named Anna had something else in mind.

"Lots of clothes are made in Vietnam. I see 'Made in Vietnam' on a lot of labels."

"Yeah, why is that?" Rebecca asked. "And China. Like everything in our house is made in China." She held up her binder. "Like this. Made in China. I mean, are we too dumb to make binders?"

"Well," Mr. Walker said, "companies in the United States figured out a long time ago that they could have their products made in those countries because they can pay the workers so much less. The laws aren't the same as they are here. The workers don't have the same rights."

"That seems wrong," I said.

Mr. Walker nodded. "Believe it or not, using so many products made in China or Vietnam or other far-off places impacts climate change, which I know interests a few of you in here." He looked at me, Rebecca, and a few other Climate Club students in the room.

"Think about it. You buy some cheap toy or T-shirt or other product that you'd find around your house. Like a binder. If it's made in the United States, it only travels a fairly short distance to the local Target or whatever. Rebecca, where was that binder bought?"

She held it up and looked at the back. "Staples."

"Okay. Or the local Staples. But when stuff is made out in East or Southeast Asia, it has to be shipped across the world to get to us. That binder is now traveling thousands of extra miles. We buy the binders, so they make more, and then the new ones have to make that same long trip. It all burns so much fuel."

"What can we even do about that?" a student asked. "Basically everything seems to be made out there."

"There's not much you can do," Mr. Walker said. "But people who are really concerned about the impact on the climate work very hard to avoid products that aren't made in North America. They read labels, learn about stores that only sell American-made products. It's an effort, but it can be done."

I made a mental note of that discussion.

As Christmas approached, the Climate Club continued its social media presence, gaining dozens of followers. As a result of the news clip, support continued to pour in from across the country—even in far-off places like Sweden, Finland, and Australia. The Sierra Club and 350.org, organizations that fight for a cleaner planet, had retweeted the story, adding supportive comments.

But it wasn't all happy stuff. One day after school, as I sat in Mr. Walker's room and waited for a Climate Club meeting to start, I noticed a comment under the original Channel 4 tweet. It referred to me by an unflattering word and suggested "those Plymouth kids" were merely seeking attention and that politicians must be using us to further some agenda.

"My grandpa probably tweeted that," I joked to Rebecca.

"Really?" she said. "It takes my grandpa fifteen minutes to find the power button on their computer."

I nearly spit out the water I had just sipped. But my amusement quickly faded when I noticed another comment. Its author apparently detected that I was biracial, even if only a quarter Cambodian.

"She should worry about her own country," the tweet read.

My own country? What did that even mean? I remembered Mom mentioning some negative, race-related comments that had been aimed at her over the years. I think she wanted to prepare me in case similar hatred was ever directed my way. But until then, I had been spared. I'm sure if my classmates were asked about it, they'd know that I wasn't the same race as them, but the difference was subtle enough that I don't know if it really registered with them.

This time I wasn't spared. I remembered how hurt I felt for Aliya that day on the beach. And yes, I had heard Mom's stories. But I never imagined I'd be the target.

Mr. Walker said he'd contact Twitter and try to get those comments removed.

I didn't stay angry at social media for long. A few days later, Ariana FaceTimed me and frantically told me to open Twitter and check the Channel 4 tweet.

"I want to see your face when you read it. You might die. I'm not even kidding."

Mom said I could quickly use her Twitter account to read the tweet. It included the following comment: "Incredible job by these kids. What's happening in East City, and other cities, is unacceptable. Fossil fuels need to be left in the ground. These companies can't get away with polluting the air our children breathe. #letECbreathe"

The tweet was from the movie star Leonardo DiCaprio.

No. Way. No way! My eyes and mouth opened as wide as I could possibly open them, but I was speechless.

"Well?" Ariana said. "Are you seeing it? Why aren't you saying anything?"

I finally composed myself enough to speak. "Is this real? Please tell me this is real!"

"It's real!"

"Oh my God!"

"I know!"

That was the start of a snowball hurtling downhill. In the coming days, more celebrities—none as big as Leonardo DiCaprio! —and politicians took up the cause.

This had officially become bigger than any of us had imagined.

Chapter

"So I got a new letter from Don today," I told Mom soon after getting home from school one afternoon, just days before the school's holiday vacation began.

"Oh yeah? Anything interesting?"

"Kinda. He wrote a lot more than normal. I guess Beth showed him the news segment. He had some advice for me."

In his letter, Don described some of his experiences during the Civil Rights Movement, which I found so interesting.

"I like to talk about it," he wrote. "But between you and me and this paper, I didn't do much."

He explained that at the time, he had a good job and was married with two young children, and he was afraid that he might get fired for his activism. Or that he could be the victim of violence while protesting.

"I regret that now," he wrote. "I wish I had been more involved. I knew the cause was so important. I knew that taking a stand was the right thing to do.

But I was a little afraid. So after my arrest, I basically stopped."

I showed Mom the letter. It was written in different-colored pens, which I assumed meant that he had not completed it in one sitting.

"I'm sure it was a lot of effort for him to write this much," Mom said. When she got to the end of the letter, she pointed to the final few sentences and asked, "Is this the advice you were talking about?"

"Yeah."

"Sounds like good advice to me. I'll bet it's motivating you already."

"Definitely."

I took the letter back and re-read the last portion of it. "Climate change is an important issue. Really important. Even if it feels like no one is listening to you, or like they think you're wrong or wasting your time, keep going. Keep fighting. You should never stop fighting for something you believe in, especially if your goal is to help people."

I felt so validated reading those words. "You should never stop." At that moment, I told myself I would follow his advice. *I'll never stop.*

The next afternoon, though, my resolve was tested. A few of us in the Climate Club were interviewed by Channel 4 right after school, delaying the start of the final Climate Club meeting before holiday vacation. Since the story about the protest had generated such interest, including celebrity support, the station decided to run a follow-up segment.

I wasn't the only student interviewed, but I guess I was the focus. This made me a little uncomfortable, since all of us were part of the protest and the work we had done. But Mr. Walker told me that because it was my interview that had received so much attention, people would probably recognize me, which is why the station wanted to do another story about us.

And since the original segment had aired, I had unwittingly received a fair amount of attention around school. I just smiled and nodded politely as students called to me in the hallway. Or when Principal Lewis referred to it on the morning announcements. Or when the art teacher jokingly asked for my autograph (so embarrassing).

Following the interview that day, those of us who participated settled into our seats to start the meeting. Mrs. Young and everyone else had been chatting and patiently waiting for us. She smiled at us and made some small talk before the meeting began.

"So, Mia," she said, "what's it been like to be getting all this attention lately?"

"I don't know. Kinda weird."

Then I—and everyone else in the meeting—heard a voice from the side of the room: "Oh please, you love it."

It was spoken softly and without eye contact by an eighth grader named Kara. And it was definitely not said in a lighthearted tone. Kara and I barely knew each other. This was not meant as a joke.

Mr. Walker and Mrs. Young furrowed their brows and glared at Kara.

"That was absolutely uncalled for," Mrs. Young said.

But Kara did not immediately back down. Continuing to look at nothing and no one in particular, she said, "Whatever. There's a whole class full of us here, but everyone talks about her like she's the only one doing anything."

I was initially stunned and unsure how to react, as I felt so many eyes fixed on me. But then, much to my dismay, emotion began to well up inside of me. I knew tears would begin to drip out of my eyes any moment, and I didn't want anyone to see that. I didn't want to become the center of attention even more than I already was. Reflexively, I got out of my chair and abruptly left the room so I could compose myself.

When I had gotten far enough away, I sat down at a table in the hallway and I started to cry. And not just a little leaking. I cried as if everything, from the night of Reggie to that day, had finally hit me—all I had learned about climate change, confronting my parents, arguing with Grandpa, skipping school with Christian, organizing a protest. Everything. I sobbed. Alone.

A minute or so later, Rebecca appeared, and while I tried to get control of my emotions, I felt a warm feeling just seeing my closest friend. She sat beside me.

"Don't listen to her," Rebecca said. "She's a jerk. She never even does anything. She made one poster, and my dog could have made a better one."

Through my crying and sniffling, I reminded her, "Your dog died like two years ago."

"Exactly my point," she said, generating a slight smile from me like only she could.

We sat together for a few minutes, and I began to compose myself. I had read the negative comments on Twitter and managed to suppress my feelings about them, but this one stung. It came from a peer, someone with whom I was, at least theoretically, working toward a common goal.

Then Aliya and Ariana approached us.

"Mr. Walker sent us out here to check on you guys," Aliya said. She looked at me. "You okay?"

"Yeah. Didn't mean to make a scene like that."

Ariana shook her head in disgust. "Um, you weren't the one who made the scene."

"I can't believe she said that," Aliya said.

"Do you think other kids feel that way, too?" I wondered aloud. "Do any of you guys?"

"No way!" My friends were reassuring. And believable.

Then Ariana delivered some news. "Matt stood up for you after you left."

"Matt?" I said. Aliya's eye roll suggested she thought this news could wait.

"Yeah! He said something like, 'I don't think Mia is looking for attention. She was getting on me about recycling before there even was a Climate Club.'"

"Whoa," Rebecca said. "He's so into you."

Just then, Mrs. Young called from just outside the classroom door. "Everything okay?"

I stood up, dabbed under my eyes, and began to walk back to the meeting.

"Everything's fine," I said. And I mostly meant it.

As I walked past Mrs. Young, she softly said, "Don't let her get to you."

"I won't."

Kara apologized to me when I returned to the room. I accepted the apology, though I assumed it was forced.

The rest of the meeting was awkward. At one point I wondered to myself, despite my friends' supportive words, if I was too involved, too eager, too outwardly passionate. If my devotion to this cause had gone far enough. Then I remembered Don's words: "Never stop fighting for something you believe in."

Kara's words had hurt, but I couldn't let them knock me off course.

Chapter

The last morning before school vacation, I walked in on a conversation that made my day.

"Hey Mom," Nate said while he ate breakfast. "Can Olivia come over for dinner tomorrow?"

The next day was December 23rd, the night of our annual Christmas Eve-Eve tradition. It was usually Uncle James's first night in town, and he would join us for a pizza dinner. Always a small gathering, it took place before the flood of relatives descended upon our house for the ensuing two days. Sometimes, Nate and I would invite a friend to the dinner. We all looked forward to that fun, relaxed night, a calm before the storm, especially for my parents.

I had just entered the kitchen in time to hear Nate's question.

"Who's Olivia?" I asked, my curiosity piqued.

Mom whipped her head around. "Whoa, Mia doesn't know yet?"

"Know what?" I said.

"Oh," Mom said, "get me some popcorn. This is gonna be good!"

Nate smiled and shook his head.

"So, who is she? Come on!" My interest level was now off the charts.

"She's my new girlfriend," Nate said. Then he resumed eating his toast.

"Oh really?" I asked. "Wait, that's all?"

"Oh no," Mom said, grinning ear to ear. "Tell her the whole story. Or I will."

Nate groaned. "Fine. She saw you on the news, and she's really into the whole climate thing, like you are."

"Oh, cool! Sounds like a smart choice," I said.

"No, wait, that's the abridged version," said Mom, who was clearly enjoying every second of this. "See, Nate's had a crush on this girl since like 8th grade...."

"Oh, here we go," Nate said, looking equal parts amused and embarrassed. Mom continued.

"So like I was saying, Nate's had a crush on her. But he was afraid to talk to her, or she had a boyfriend, or she seemed to not notice him. Or whatever. But then a couple of weeks ago, she comes up to him all excited and says, 'Your sister is amazing, she's so cute, I totally agree with her,' the whole thing. And they start talking, Nate took a chance, and now they're a couple! Can you believe that?"

"So what you're saying," I said, "is that I, by being so awesome, got you a date with this girl you've been crushing on, and you haven't screwed it up yet?"

Nate seemed mildly offended. "I wouldn't put it that way."

"I would!" Mom fired back, and she high-fived me while we both laughed hysterically.

Nate interrupted the good-natured teasing at his expense. "So, is it okay if she comes over or not?"

"Of course it is!" Mom declared.

Nate then turned to me. "She seriously does want to meet you, though."

I did meet Olivia at the pizza dinner, which was also attended by Rebecca and Ariana—Aliya had other plans. "I would love to help you guys," Olivia told them. "Nobody listens to me when I talk about the climate. My friends think I've been brainwashed. I wish we had a club at the high school like the one you have."

I had to wait a little longer for Uncle James to finally arrive; he took the train from Chicago, a trip that began the night before and took nearly twenty-four hours. But he had sworn off air travel because of its environmental impact.

"Planes just burn a crazy amount of fuel," he had said when we talked on the phone a few days earlier.

"You flew back with me in September," I had protested.

"I made an exception. I didn't want to subject you to a twenty-one-hour train ride."

I was slightly annoyed. "I totally would have done it. You guys protect me too much."

Uncle James laughed. "You're twelve!"

"Thirteen in a few weeks," I reminded him.

That night he brought some news about the ongoing effort in East City to halt the proposed expansion of the oil refinery. After several protests and meetings, EurOil, the company that owned the refinery, had agreed to delay the decision about expanding its facility to support more tar sands. That wasn't a victory by any means, but it wasn't a defeat. At least not yet.

"It just means we have to keep fighting," he told us.

"Why does it keep happening to that one place?" Rebecca asked.

Uncle James sighed. "The reality is, East City is a largely minority city. A good part of the population is Black and Latino. There's a long history in our country of the dirtiest factories, the worst air quality, the most polluted water, being found in minority communities. And governments have mostly allowed the pollution to happen. They just look the other way."

Mom had joined us in the living room halfway through the conversation.

"I'm forty-five years old, and I've lived in America my whole life," she said. "And I never really knew that. I feel ashamed, honestly."

"We've been fortunate enough to live where we have," Uncle James said. "But there's this whole other world out there, in our own country. It is hard to believe at times."

He turned to my friends and me. "Keep up the pressure on social media. People really started to notice. They need to know that it isn't over yet."

"We will," I said. "What else can we do?"

"I don't know. But I'm sure you guys and your teachers will come up with something."

Then Rebecca looked at Mom. "Wait," she said. "You're forty-five? You're like seven years older than my mom! You look *way* younger."

Mom smiled and shook her head. "Thanks, I think?"

My whole family, including all four of my grand-parents and my uncle, enjoyed a happy and relatively uneventful Christmas. Grandpa and I got along fine, essentially pretending that our disagreement back in November had never happened, even though I periodically replayed parts of it in my mind.

I did notice very little conversation between Grandpa and Uncle James. After everyone had gone home, I asked Dad about that.

"Yeah, they don't really see eye to eye about a lot of things," he said.

"Like what?"

"I don't want to get into it too much. But you saw how Grandpa reacted to your opinions about climate change. He has very strong views on some things. And so does Uncle James. They clash a lot, and sometimes it's gotten a little heated between them. I think they both kind of figured out that the less they talk, the more peaceful it'll be. Which is unfortunate, really. They're father and son."

"I never noticed that before. Has it always been like that?"

"For several years. Most of your life, actually. I guess they've hidden it pretty well. But now, as you grow up, you're more perceptive."

He paused and seemed to be considering how to word what he wanted to say next.

"I don't agree with your uncle on some things. And I don't agree with your grandfather on some things. But I could never imagine risking my relationship with either of them because of some differences of opinion. I think they both want the other person to see their side. I don't know why that matters so much."

In a weird way, I felt like I *did* know why it mattered. "Well," I said, "if the other side is harmful to people, then wouldn't you want people to agree with you?"

Dad smiled. "Your uncle has said stuff like that before. No wonder you two have always gotten along so well."

Christmas night, after all guests had left—except for Uncle James, who was staying at our house—I was glued to my phone, texting with Christian. Some of his texts made me laugh out loud, and then I'd quickly return to rapidly typing out my response.

"What's so funny over there?" Uncle James had asked me.

"Nothing. Just texting one of my friends."

Nate happened to be walking behind the couch on which I was sitting, so he spied the name on my phone.

"She's texting Christian. I think it's her boyfriend."

"Boyfriend?" Uncle James asked. "And I don't know about him?"

I didn't take my eyes off the phone, but I certainly heard Nate. "He's not my boyfriend. Ignore him. Nate's just jealous because he needed me to get him his girlfriend."

"Please," Nate retorted. "They skipped school together to go to a protest in Boston."

Dad overheard us from the kitchen. "All right! Let's not rehash this again."

"Okay," Uncle James said. "But this is a lot for me here. A boy? Protest? Skipping school? I'm gonna need details eventually."

I barely noticed his words. I had already returned my attention to my phone. And Christian.

I officially became a teenager on January seventeenth, the day after Martin Luther King Jr. Day. When I got to school, I opened my locker and found a typed note inside—a small sheet of paper folded in half to resemble a card. It was colorful, with lots of hand-drawn balloons. There were only two typed words: Happy birthday!

Happy birthday? I almost never talked about my birthday. I was sure that I could count on one hand the number of kids in the school who knew it was my birthday. I slipped the note into my backpack. Then Rebecca walked by on her way to homeroom.

"Hey Becks, did you tell anyone today's my birthday?"

"I don't think so. I mean, I talked to Ari and Aliya about it, since we're coming to your house today. But no one was around us, I don't think."

I shrugged. "Okay."

"Why?"

I showed the note to Rebecca, who examined it closely.

"It's typed," she noted. "Do you think it's from the same person?"

"I have no idea."

I had other things on my mind anyway. That day, an environmental activist named William Klein was scheduled to speak to a whole-school assembly in the auditorium. Mr. Walker had told us that he wanted to book someone who could open the eyes of the entire student population to how humans were impacting the environment. After all, while thirty-six students had joined the Climate Club, that meant several hundred had not.

Once the Channel 4 news clip had aired, a few potential guest speakers returned Mr. Walker's emails. Mr. Klein had informed Mr. Walker that he had a conference the previous weekend in Boston, so he agreed to stick around an extra couple of days and address the students. He would waive his typical speaking fee, he said. Perhaps, Mr. Walker had told us at our last meeting—the *Kara* meeting—a captivating speech from a man considered an expert on climate change would resonate with the kids.

And that's exactly what happened. The students were riveted by the presentation. Mr. Klein's slide-show included photos of animals searching for their homes in deforested lands; sea life tangled in plastic; polar bears clinging to one last chunk of sea ice; golden frogs, nearly extinct, living in special tanks instead of out in the wild; Chinese citizens wearing masks and surrounded by smog-filled air; an African family standing beside drooping crops as the land around them resembled the sand at a Plymouth beach.

When Mr. Klein paused to take a breath or

advance his slide presentation, the auditorium was quiet enough that a pin dropping would have startled the audience. I was hanging on every word.

Making the day even more memorable, Mr. Klein, a skinny guy with a mixture of gray and dark brown hair who was probably about ten years older than my dad, offered to have lunch with the Climate Club in Mr. Walker's room after the assembly. We would get to talk with someone who had dedicated his life to climate change!

"I've been so inspired by how you have supported the people of East City," he told us. "We need more of you around the country to take a stand like that. Too many kids, I think, are afraid of what people might think of them. Not everyone is willing to put themselves out there for a cause. You should be commended."

"We're awesome," Rebecca blurted out, which sparked laughter and served to relax all of us.

We asked several questions about Mr. Klein's activism and the future health of the planet. I had a specific question about something he had mentioned during his talk.

"You mentioned something about a sixth extinction? What did you mean?"

He nodded. "Well, some scientists believe we're in the middle of a sixth mass extinction. There have been five throughout the history of life on the planet. Something would happen to make it hard to live on Earth, and many living things would go extinct. Like sixty-six million years ago, when an asteroid hit and wiped out the dinosaurs and many other species. Normally, it's very rare for a species to go extinct. But now, it's happening fairly often. We're losing lots of animal species, and humans are to blame."

"Wow, that's depressing," Rebecca said.

"Do you ever feel like nothing will ever be done about it?" Christian asked. "Do you ever feel like giving up?"

"I will never give up on this," Mr. Klein said. "Yes, it sometimes feels like we're running on a treadmill, burning our energy and getting nowhere. Giving a lot of effort and very little reward. But eventually, things will change. They'll have to. I want to help things to change as quickly as possible, because I believe that will lead to a better future for everyone.

"And some communities are doing amazing work, moving toward zero emissions. Your state, in fact, is generating a lot of solar and wind power. If I have one thing that I hope you will get from this, it's that giving up is the worst thing you can do. Keep doing what you're doing. Keep at it. Don't give up. It's your futures that we're all fighting for. A lot of young people have gotten involved, but there needs to be many, many more."

When the lunch bell rang, we all stood and gathered our things to bring to our next class. We thanked Mr. Klein.

"No, really, thank you," he said. "For all you're doing."

I was so inspired.

That evening, after my friends had visited and brought me brownies, my basketball team won our game, capping a memorable birthday and leaving me super upbeat as Mom drove us home.

"You guys were on fire tonight," Mom told me on the ride home.

"I think that was our best game of the season," I said.

"I don't think I've ever seen Rebecca play that good. Did she miss one shot all night?"

"Now that you mention it, I don't think she did! And she got like every rebound, too."

Mom laughed. "Maybe it was the brownies you two ate before the game. You both played on a sugar high."

As we pulled into their driveway, we noticed Beth approaching our front door. Beth spotted the car and, rather than ringing the doorbell, waited for us.

"Hi Beth!" I said, hopping out of the car and wondering what type of news she was about to tell us.

"Hey! I came by to get my dad's mail, and I wanted to stop over before I head back."

"How is your dad?" Mom asked.

"Honestly, he's doing great. That's what I wanted to tell you. His legs have healed pretty well, and he's working his butt off to get them strong again. Everyone is so impressed with his progress. He seems to be exceeding their expectations over there."

"That's awesome!" I said.

"Yeah," Mom added, "that's really great news. We're so glad to hear it!"

"Does this mean he could move back home?" I asked.

"We don't know that yet," Beth said. "He still has a long way to go. And part of me still thinks it's a bad idea. But he's determined, and that determination is really helping him get better."

Beth looked at me. "I didn't think, at his age, that he'd be able to handle this rehab. I've seen him doing it; it's pretty intense. But I know how much he cares about you guys, and that he loves living here. It's his home."

The three of us said our goodbyes, then Mom and I scurried inside, out of the January cold. As we closed the front door behind us and I started to remove my coat, the kitchen lights suddenly turned on, revealing Dad and Nate in very cheap, sparkly, purple party hats.

"Surprise!" Dad yelled. Nate said it too, but from him, it was more of a groan.

I was touched just the same. "Aw, thanks guys!"

"Oh, it was the least we could do," Dad said. "And we made you a little cake." He lifted it off the counter and placed it on the kitchen table. It was chocolate. I looked at it closely. I was appreciative, yet horrified. So was Mom.

"It's shaped like a," Mom said, "like a—"

"Like a rhombus," Nate interjected. "We know. We think it tastes good, though. You always say it's what's on the inside that counts."

"Exactly," said Dad, "now let's eat dinner so we can devour this cake before it topples over."

All of that excitement, plus even more sugar, helped keep me awake past my usual bedtime. Nate didn't help; he popped into my room around 9:30.

"Hey, someone told me that an eighth-grader at your school got caught with drugs," he said. "Do you know about that? Have you heard anything?"

"No," I said. "Nothing. Do you know who it was?"

"No," he said. "Maybe it's just a rumor."

I paid attention enough in health class to know that drugs were bad and all, but I always figured I was too young for that to even be on my radar. Not anymore, apparently.

I couldn't fall asleep for what seemed like at least an hour after I finally went to bed. So I took a break from staring at the ceiling to grab my phone off the end table. I fired off a text to Uncle James, who had left me a happy birthday voicemail earlier in the day.

"Any news on East City?"

"Not really," he wrote back. "Still waiting."

"OK. Keep me posted."

"I will. Hey, I know you're thirteen now, but shouldn't you be asleep?"

"Yes. Good night."

"Good night, Mimi."

Chapter

One Thursday night in the first week of February, Mom knocked on my bedroom door and then opened it before I even had a chance to speak.

Mom had been in the living room preparing for a job interview scheduled for the next morning in Boston. It was a public relations job, and she said that she felt qualified for it, but it didn't excite her in any way. Still, she told me, a paycheck was a paycheck.

While researching the company that had invited her to interview, she got sidetracked by a news headline that brought her to a *Chicago Tribune* story. That's why she zipped up to my room.

The article was short and to the point. It began like this:

EAST CITY, Ind.—Protests against a proposed expansion of the Blackstone Oil Refinery, which have been a regular occurrence in this city in recent months, led to several arrests for the first time on Wednesday.

The protesters have increased in numbers recently, but the gatherings have remained without incident. The plight of this city has garnered some national attention, leading parent company EurOil to delay a final decision on the proposal. Residents have continued to protest, and on Wednesday night, five were arrested on Blackstone grounds after they refused to disperse when ordered to do so by police.

My jaw dropped. This seemed like huge news! I also thought about my friends. "Do you think Hector and Tracey are safe?"

"I'm sure they're fine," Mom said. "Some arrests aren't unusual in protests. Sometimes people get arrested on purpose, to bring attention to their cause. But these were the first arrests there. I wonder if that will be a one-time thing, or if everything will change there now."

Early the following week, after Mom returned to Boston for a second interview, the two of us spoke to Uncle James. He told us that the citizens of East City had become more organized in their protest efforts, and that some had, in fact, agreed to endure arrest in the hope that it would attract more attention. Others had followed their lead a couple of days later.

"They're hoping to force the issue," he told us. "They're tired of getting the run-around."

As it turned out, Mom did not get the public relations job. I was disappointed for her—even if she was ambivalent about the job to begin with—but selfishly happy that I'd continue seeing more of her.

In the days and weeks that followed, I noticed that she was often reading a new library book, always about the climate in some way. This led to conversations about food production, ice in the Arctic, the importance of glaciers, rising sea levels, and use of pesticides and other chemicals in the United States. She was teaching me new things every day. She even arranged for us to lease solar panels for the roof of our house, starting us on the path away from fossil fuels.

I now had a partner at home. We talked about climate change so much, sharing our knowledge with each other and growing closer than ever.

One evening, curious about the progress in East City, we FaceTimed Uncle James.

"There was a big meeting out there this morning, actually," he told us. "We were there. So were city leaders and a lot of other groups who are trying to help them. And a lot of angry citizens."

"Has any progress been made?" I asked.

"No. But next Sunday, we're planning the biggest protest yet. The goal is to get as many residents of East City and surrounding areas as possible. I'm one of the organizers, basically trying to recruit people from my city. I'm explaining to them how much this pollution affects them, too."

Mom looked at me. Then back at the phone.

"Next Sunday?" she asked.

"Yeah. The nineteenth."

"Okay. Well, thanks for the update. Good luck!"

After ending the call, the wheels in her mind clearly turning, she looked back at me with an excited look on her face.

"Why do you keep looking at me like that?" I asked.

"The protest is the nineteenth."

"Yeah. So?"

"Doesn't February vacation start the eighteenth? How would you feel about going?"

"Are you serious?" I nearly leapt off the couch.

"I think we should do this," Mom said. "You've already been involved so much. And I feel like I need to step up here."

I threw my arms around her with such force that both of us nearly lost our balance. I had never even considered that we could do something like this!

"Now here's the thing," Mom said. "We can't really afford plane tickets right now, and —

I cut her off. "We shouldn't fly anyway."

"I agree. I'll drive if I have to, but I'll look and see if the train is affordable."

I was giddy. It was probably the most excited I'd been since, well, the last time I found out I'd be going to Chicago. Of course, this trip was for a very different reason.

Then I had a thought.

"Can Rebecca come with us?" I asked.

Mom pondered my request. "Let me talk to her mom first. That way, if her mom doesn't want her to, then Rebecca won't get her hopes up."

As it turned out, Rebecca's mom gave her approval, and Uncle James enthusiastically offered his apartment for the three of us to stay. Mom booked the train tickets—we would leave Friday and travel through the night, and then we'd return the following Thursday. In the middle, we'd attend a major protest against industrial pollution in East City.

What other seventh graders could say that?

Chapter

The day before the train trip to Chicago, which was a Thursday, I was sitting in science class, halfway through the period just prior to lunch. As I listened to Mrs. Young's instructions about a time capsule project, I saw Christian pass by my classroom. We waved to each other, and then I returned my focus to Mrs. Young.

But then things got really weird.

The previous week, a new rumor had spread around the school of a student bringing drugs in the building. No one seemed to know who, or if it was even true. I had asked Nate if he had heard that rumor too, like the one he had mentioned to me on my birthday, and he had, from a friend with a younger sister at my school.

"Have you ever tried any drugs?" I asked him, curious but also afraid to learn the answer.

"No," he said. "I'd be too scared to get kicked off the lacrosse team. Coach Wilson said if anyone gets caught with drugs, they're gone." After a brief pause, he casually mentioned, "I know kids who have, though."

The issue began to spread around the middle school, to the point that Principal Lewis delivered a firm message earlier that week during the morning announcements.

"If anyone is found to have any illegal drug, you will be suspended, and that suspension will go on your record."

So by the morning of my time capsule project, the school was on high alert.

Much of what happened over the next few hours was later explained to me by Christian and some of my other friends. It apparently all started when a seventh-grade girl named Savanna exited the bathroom and noticed, from a distance, a boy dropping something through the vents of a locker down the hall.

My locker.

Savanna, remembering a lecture about the importance of reporting any concerning behavior, informed her teacher of what she had seen. Her teacher notified the office, and the principals viewed the security footage. They identified Christian as the student Savanna had spotted, so they called Christian's classroom and had him sent to the office.

It was a total coincidence that the school had already decided on a plan to resolve the drug thing. On that very day. So as I was writing my time capsule letter and Christian sat nervously in an assistant principal's office, Principal Lewis made an announcement to the entire school:

"This is a shelter-in-place. Please remain in your classroom."

Teachers closed and locked their doors. At that time, unbeknownst to me, town police officers moved through the school's hallways with dogs trained to sniff for drugs.

It all seemed a little intense for middle school.

The shelter-in-place was lifted before lunch, but when my friends and I took our usual seats in the cafeteria, Christian wasn't there.

Nothing suspicious had turned up in any of the lockers—mine included—around where Christian was seen on the security footage. Principal Lewis and Mr. Jones, one of the assistant principals, assumed that whatever he'd placed in a locker was now in the hands of the locker's owner. They insisted that Christian reveal everything: What did he place in the locker? And whose locker was it?

Christian insisted that he had brought no drugs into school, that day or ever. The principals demanded to know what he *had* slid into a locker. He refused to say.

Finally, when they threatened to call his parents, he confessed. He left a note. In my locker.

Apparently the principals were skeptical.

"If that's all it is, then why wouldn't you tell us? You've been acting like you're hiding something."

"Because," Christian said, "she doesn't know."

"Doesn't know what? Won't she see the note?"

"Yes."

But Christian wouldn't say anymore, and an exasperated Principal Lewis turned to Mr. Jones. "Am I missing something?"

Mr. Jones, apparently figuring out what was going on, whispered in the principal's ear. Her eyes widened, and she looked back at Christian. Her intensity softened. It all made sense to her now.

"Listen," she said. "You're a good kid. So is Mia. You've never caused us any problems before. Except for that whole skipping school thing." She smirked. "But I'm gonna need to confirm with Mia that there was a note in her locker and nothing else. So it looks like you're gonna have to fess up to her."

That's when I heard the following words on a two-way radio belonging to a teacher on lunch duty: "Please send Mia Dubois to my office."

I arrived in the principal's office a few minutes later, having left the cafeteria in the middle of lunch. Principal Lewis met me at her office.

"Have a seat," she said. "I think this will be quick."

I was sweating. While I was confident I had done nothing wrong, this all seemed ominous. Getting summoned by the principal was not familiar to me, and my mind raced to try to remember if I had somehow messed up without even realizing it.

"Was there a note in your locker today?" Principal Lewis asked me.

"A note?"

"Yeah. Possibly a note from someone who didn't identify himself?"

The secret admirer note?

"Oh. Yeah. I've gotten some of those this year." Was I in trouble for receiving anonymous notes?

"Should I have told you about them?" I asked.

"No. But can you show me the one you got today?"

I was confused by this fairly relaxed interrogation from the principal, but I conveyed none of that. "Okay. It's in one of my binders in science."

"Let's go then."

I walked down the hall to Mrs. Young's classroom, escorted by Principal Lewis. My books and binders were on the floor, so I squatted down, opened the binder I used for homework, and pulled the note out of the inside pouch.

I handed it to the principal, who quickly examined it. Then she gave it back to me. I returned it to my binder.

"And you have no idea who put that in your locker?"

"No."

I noticed that she fought back a smile. I wondered if the principal knew who wrote the note, but I felt too embarrassed to ask, and too eager to be done with this whole awkward situation.

"I'm sure you're wondering what this is all about," she said. "We had a report of a student slipping something into your locker. With all that's been going on around here, there were concerns that it might be something that doesn't belong in our school. It turned out to be that note. You just provided the proof that cleared the student who's been writing you those notes."

She flashed a mischievous smile. "I'll just leave it at that."

I told Aliya about the strange incident during our bus ride home, but beyond that, I hoped to just forget about it. That afternoon, however, as I sat in the living room with Mom, the doorbell rang.

I opened the door. It was Christian.

"Hey! What are you doing here?" I asked him.

"I just want to talk to you about something. Can you come out?"

"It's freezing! You can come in." I noticed his bike.

"You rode your bike over here? It's like negative twenty out there." I was exaggerating, but it really was cold!

"Just put on a coat or something," Christian implored me. "I have to tell you something. It won't take long."

I looked at him quizzically. Then I got my coat off the couch. "Mom, it's Christian. I'm going outside for a minute."

"Okay," Mom said.

As I walked out the door and toward the driveway where Christian was waiting, I glanced back at the house and noticed Mom peeking through the window in my room. I guess she was still a little suspicious of him, what with the Boston trip and all. And then, all of a sudden, I began to piece things together. Was Christian the secret admirer? Why else would he have come to my house?

Still, I avoided outwardly jumping to conclusions until I heard what he had to say.

"What's going on?" I asked. "You're kinda freaking me out a little."

It felt like a conversation that required sitting, but there was nowhere to sit in the front yard, other than the cold, hard ground. So we stood.

"There's something I've wanted to tell you for, like, months. But I kept chickening out." He must have been super nervous because he wouldn't even look at me. Instead, he stared down at his right Adidas sneaker, which nudged around a gray rock about the size of a golf ball.

"Okay," I said, equally nervous as I quickly tried to think of the right response in case he said what I was expecting he would. "What is it?"

There was an uncomfortable pause. Finally, he spoke.

"It's me who has been writing you those notes this year."

Even though I had been preparing for that revelation, it was still jarring to hear him speak the words. It gave me a strange fuzzy feeling in my belly.

"You? Really? Why didn't you say something?"

Christian finally looked at me. "Can't you see how weird this is?"

I found myself rapidly reviewing the timeline of events in my head.

"Wait, the first few notes were before we even knew each other."

"I know. But I had seen you around last year and all. And at that basketball game."

"And some were written and others were typed?"

"I was afraid you might have figured out my handwriting."

I was definitely flattered, even if the whole situation was noticeably awkward. I wanted to say the right things, but I had no experience to call upon. This was a conversation unlike any other in my thirteen years.

"So, like, you think I'm cute?" I asked, scrunching up my nose. I had only really been called "cute" by grown-ups. "My smile? My eyes? You have a crush on me?"

Christian, back to his game of soccer with the rock, said, "It shouldn't be that surprising. I mean, I went to Boston with you."

"Yeah. But I thought that was because of how much you care about climate change."

"No, it is. I do. But I wouldn't have just skipped school and gone to a protest with Matt O'Connor."

This made me laugh, something he was pretty good at doing. And I was beginning to feel happy about this major development. Unsure how to act or what to say, but happy.

"Well, I'm glad it was you," I said.

"Really?" Christian perked up.

"Well, yeah. I mean, I've always found boys mostly gross and annoying. And whenever my friends guessed who they thought might be writing the notes, I always hoped they weren't right. But now that I know it's you, I'm glad."

"So I'm not gross and annoying?" Christian was serious but trying to make me laugh at the same time.

"Not as much," I said, my efforts to maintain a straight face failing.

"So we're still friends, right?" Christian asked rhetorically.

"I guess." We smiled and looked at each other. I wasn't sure how to proceed in that moment, and it seemed Christian wasn't, either. Finally Christian said, "Well, I'm freezing. I think I'm gonna go back home."

I then realized that I could barely feel my fingers.

"Okay. I'll see you tomorrow," I said.

"Yeah. You kinda have a big day tomorrow."

"Yeah." Right, Chicago. I had momentarily forgotten that I'd be on a train in a little more than twenty-four hours.

"Okay, see ya," he said.

"Bye."

I waited until Christian was down the road a bit. Then I turned and walked back in the house, feverishly rubbing my frozen hands together and unable to suppress a smile.

Mom, sitting on the couch and acting as if she hadn't been spying on me, asked matter-of-factly, "Everything all right?"

"Yeah."

"What was that all about?"

"It's kind of a long story."

Just then, we heard a car door close. I looked out the window and saw that Nate was home.

"Well then," her mom said, "why don't you tell me all about it tomorrow on the trip. No story is too long for a twenty-one-hour train ride."

"Sounds like a plan."

That night after dinner, I took a break from packing for the trip, bounded downstairs, and headed toward the kitchen to refill my glass with water. As I passed through the dining room, I saw Dad standing behind the table, staring out the back window.

It was dark outside, though Dad had flipped on the backyard floodlights. He said nothing at first.

"Everything all right, Dad?"

"Yeah. Ready for your trip?"

"Yup. I'm pretty excited."

"That's great, sweetie."

I thought he was acting strange. "Dad?"

"Yeah?"

"What are you doing?"

"I love looking at those pines when it's a little windy."

Beyond our backyard was a wooded area, and almost every tree was a majestic pine, at least seventy feet tall. Just like the one that had fallen from the corner of our yard and crashed onto our deck and into our kitchen.

"You see how those trees seem to sway, almost like they're dancing together? I find it so peaceful to watch them," he said.

I stood beside him and looked through the window. Whenever I'd hear the breeze pick up, I'd notice the pine trees would intensify their swaying. Their dancing.

Dad shook his head. "I still can't believe those trees caused us and Don so much damage the night of the hurricane."

"I know," I said. "Me either."

Our deck was still not fixed, something plainly obvious as we looked out the window. An insurance agent had inspected the damage, and Mom and Dad received a check to pay for it. But then winter hit, and the job had been put off.

"I never would have thought to cut those trees down," Dad continued. "I don't consider myself a nature freak or anything, but I love those trees. It's like they're part of living here. They were some of the first things I noticed before we bought this house. I feel like I should have anticipated that one could reach our house and put us in danger."

I sensed that he was beating himself up for what happened the night of Reggie. "It's not your fault, Dad. And none of us got hurt. We're all fine."

"I know, sweetie," he replied. "Thankfully. But with you and Mom getting so involved in this climate change thing, it's making me wonder if I should have paid closer attention to it before. You know? I can't say I'm totally sold on all of this stuff you tell me, but some of it makes sense. Maybe I just didn't want to see it before."

His admission took me by surprise, but in a good way. All I could think to say was, "It's all right, Dad."

He continued to stare out the window. "I hope we don't see another storm like that for a long time," he said.

I nodded. "Me too."

Chapter

I stood by the front door with Mom and Rebecca, waiting for Dad to grab his phone and keys so he could drive us to Boston's South Station.

"All right, Nate, I'll see you in a couple of hours," Dad said. "And since they'll be gone, we'll have steak for dinner tonight. And sliders as appetizers. With a side of beef stew."

He looked at me and Mom with a mischievous smile. I wasn't amused.

"Just further proof," Mom said to me, "that they'd be doomed without us around." Then Mom and Dad looked at each other.

"All set?"

"All set."

The Amtrak trip took us by Albany and Buffalo and Cleveland, on the way to Chicago's nearly hundred-year-old Union Station. A good part of the trip took place in the dark, limiting our views of the Great Lakes region we passed through. We did notice snow on the ground in parts of upstate New York and Ohio; it hadn't snowed much in Plymouth that winter.

I told Mom and Rebecca all about Christian, from the first anonymous letter to the Climate Club and Thursday's reveal.

Mom listened intently and didn't ask any questions until my story was over. Then she asked the most awkward question: "So, are you guys, you know, an item?"

I looked at her like she was at least seventy-five years old. "An *item*?"

"Yeah. You know. A couple. Dating."

"No!" I shrieked.

Rebecca couldn't resist. "She won't admit it, but they basically have been for months."

"Hey!" I laughed and scolded Rebecca simultaneously. "It's not *like* that. We're friends."

"It sounds like he wants to be your boyfriend," Mom said.

"Ew, Mom, stop!"

"Mia, you're thirteen. It's all right to admit that boys don't all have cooties."

Rebecca nodded in agreement. "I've been telling her this for, like, ever. She's just being stubborn. She totally likes him."

You know when your mom looks at you in a way that seems to be demanding the truth? That's what Mom did.

"Fine," I said. "I guess I kind of like him. I mean, I like him as a friend. He's really nice. It's just weird to say. I don't want someone calling me their girlfriend. No thanks."

"I get it," Mom said. "There's certainly no need to put labels on anything at your age."

"That's fine," Rebecca said, "but I'm still gonna make fun of you. Whatever you guys call yourselves."

Mom smiled. "You're not helping, Rebecca."

"Yeah, Becks," I said. "Not helping."

The only other serious topic of conversation on the train was the actual reason for the trip—Sunday's protest. We all expressed some nervous excitement for the event. I actually had the most experience in attending climate protests, even though I had been to just two.

"I said this to Rebecca's mom, and I'll say it to you both: We will be supporters of this protest, but we'll be watching more than participating. Never leave our sight. Got it?"

"Yes, got it."

"I'm especially talking to you, Mia," Mom said. "I know how passionate you are about this. But you have to remember that you're thirteen. I don't want you to get carried away."

I had been staring out the window as I listened. I nodded, but I wasn't sure if I really meant it. Like she said, I was thirteen. But sometimes she talked to me like I was eight.

When we weren't talking on the train, we passed time by reading, listening to music on our phones, playing a couple of rounds of cards, and sleeping a bit. By mid-afternoon, we had arrived in Chicago, bleary-eyed, one day before the protest.

Uncle James met us at Union Station, a large building that felt as much like a museum as a train station.

"Can we go to Gino's East for dinner, Uncle James?" I asked within minutes of greeting him with a big hug.

"You read my mind," he said.

I enjoyed some calorie-packed Chicago-style pizza,

but I—like Mom and Rebecca—was functioning on minimal sleep. So we went back to Uncle James's apartment in Ravenswood right after dinner and crashed.

The next day would be a big one. We all needed rest.

Chapter

I was the first to wake up the following morning. I was so ready for this. I showered, got dressed, and sat in the kitchen where I looked at a book, not a word of it penetrating my preoccupied mind.

Uncle James emerged from his room soon after and took a seat across from me at the kitchen table.

"Now remember, stick with us today. We need to be able to see you …"

"I know, I know. Mom told me." *Another lecture?*

"And she's right. She told me about Boston, you know."

"So she's gonna hold that over me until I'm fifty, isn't she," I said, rolling my eyes.

"Listen, I expect everything will be fine today. But people are angry."

"I'm angry too."

"I know you are. But this is their lives. Every day, being forced to breathe that air, feeling like they have no voice, like no one listens. Your life is much easier in a lot of ways. I respect you more than you know for caring this much, to come all the way out here, and all that you've done. Just remember that the people of that city are fighters, and this is their fight. We're here to support them. Don't let your emotions take over." He looked at me closely. "Okay?"

"Okay," I said. But I still wasn't sure if I had answered with total honesty.

The unofficial start to the protest seemed to be about one o'clock, but people were going to arrive when they arrived. Several of the organizations that were involved used Lincoln Elementary School as a base, so that's where Uncle James drove us at mid-morning on an unseasonably mild yet overcast day.

At about noon, while standing outside of the school, I felt a tap on my right shoulder. I quickly swung my head around and broke out into a huge smile. I threw my arms around Hector, someone with whom I had spent only a few hours in my life but felt like I knew intimately. Hector hugged me back.

"I can't believe you came all the way out here for this!" he said.

"I kinda can't either! But I'm so glad I'm here!"

Hector glanced at Mom and Rebecca, who had responded to the commotion by quickly surrounding us. From the other side, Tracey, who had stopped to chat with someone, caught up.

"This is my mom and my best friend from home, Rebecca. Guys, this is Hector."

"I've heard a lot about you, Hector," Mom said. Hector smiled and nodded.

"It's amazing that you girls did that protest at your school," Tracey said. "And the news video! That got so much attention!"

Just then, a nearby woman and high school-aged girl, having heard Tracey, flung their heads around and fixed their eyes on me.

"You're the one from that video?" the girl said. "From Massachusetts?"

"Well, let me come on over and give you a hug," said the woman. She came over and put her right arm around my shoulders. "My daughter and I sent that clip to everyone we knew. And then Leonardo DiCaprio tweeted it?" She chuckled. "Can you get me his number?"

I smiled, a bit embarrassed. "I just hope they agree not to expand the oil refinery," I said.

The woman closed her eyes and nodded. "From your lips to God's ears."

I could feel the anticipation building as one o'clock closed in. East City is a city of less than thirty thousand people, about half as many people as Plymouth. However, East City, geographically much smaller, certainly *feels* more populated, especially considering that the massive city of Chicago is just on the other side of the state line. That afternoon, to my eyes, it seemed like the entire population of Indiana was stuffed into a few blocks in the city's northeast.

Rebecca and I held signs. Mine read, "Clean air for every child;" Rebecca used the familiar "#letECbreathe." We diligently stayed toward the back as the crowd, which included many symbolically wearing masks, pushed its way north, beyond State Road, along train tracks known for transporting petcoke.

A few of the city leaders walked with the protesters. Uncle James said there had been a split among the politicians in East City. The expansion of Blackstone would lead to more jobs. More jobs would mean a stronger local and state economy, which could generate more money for the city. Plus, he said, Blackstone wasn't leaving no matter what, so some didn't want to pick a fight with a business that already provided many jobs in their city.

Other politicians, though, had apparently reached—or long since surpassed—their breaking point. The city needed less oil and lead and coal and petcoke—not more.

Suddenly, as we all briskly walked, a bunch of young adults arrived, as if they had just been let out of a bus. There appeared to be two hundred of them, maybe more. Not all of them were white, but enough of them were that it did not appear to be a group from East City.

"Who are they?" I asked Uncle James.

"Not sure," he said. "Must be activists."

The group settled into the flow of foot traffic not far from us.

"We should go ask them who they are?" Rebecca said.

"What? Won't that be awkward? What would we say?"

"I don't know. 'Who are you?'"

"You can't just say that!"

"Of course I can."

Rebecca began walking toward them. I followed anxiously. "Wait for me!"

We approached the edge of this newly formed perimeter of activists, where two guys were talking. Rebecca didn't hesitate.

"Hey," she said to them.

"Hey," they said, smiling at us.

"So, like, who are you guys?"

Both of them laughed. "Well, I'm Greg. This is Evan. And who are you?"

"We're Rebecca and Mia. And we're wondering why you're here."

They seemed to find Rebecca amusing. "We're here because we want to help get rid of fossil fuels," Greg said.

I finally spoke up. "Where are you from?"

"I'm from St. Louis and Evan is from Seattle, but we both go to college at Notre Dame. We're really involved in groups that are fighting to change climate policies."

"Cool!" I said.

"Wait a minute!" Evan said, looking at me. "Don't I know you?"

"Umm, I don't think so."

"No, I know who you are. You were in that news video! You're from Massachusetts, right?"

"Yeah, that's her!" Rebecca exclaimed.

"Rebecca and I started a climate club at our school," I said. "We held a protest for East City."

"Ohh, we all saw that video and sent it to a lot of people on campus," Greg said. "You guys are inspiring!"

"We're kind of inspired by you," Rebecca said.

"Yeah," I added. "It's nice to know so many people are interested in this. We don't always feel that way."

"It's the younger generation like us," Evan said, pointing back and forth between himself and Rebecca and me. "It's our futures. And people in government seem to mostly not care much. So it has to be us if we want things to change."

This reminded me of a similar message I received from Tess and Ava in Boston. Then it occurred to me that Rebecca and I were straying a bit from Mom and Uncle James. I didn't need any more lectures, or to be stuck in my room for the next five years. "We should get back with our family," I reluctantly said.

"Nice to meet you guys," Rebecca said.

"Yeah, you too!" Greg said. "Keep up the good work!"

At about 2:15, like a swarm of ants reaching drips of strawberry ice cream on a driveway, the marching crowd descended upon the west entrance of the oil refinery. We were toward the back, but those in the front came face to face with the police, who insisted the protest would continue no farther. The protesters obliged, but they did not disperse. They held their signs, chanted "Let us breathe! Let us breathe!" and "Keep it in the ground! Keep it in the ground!" Occasionally someone would passionately encourage the crowd to stay strong, and they would respond with deafening cheers.

Call-and-response sequences energized the gathering as well.

"Are we ready to give up?"

"No!"

"Are we going back home?"

"No!"

"Does East City need more oil?"

"No!"

"Do we deserve to breathe clean air?"

"Yes!"

From the back of the crowd, I watched with amazement at the determination of the protesters. I understood, at that moment, what Uncle James meant that morning. It was *their* protest first. They lived with polluted air every day. I had lived in a sheltered world my whole life. My problems now seemed trivial, almost embarrassingly so. The people of the city wanted what my friends and I took for granted: cleaner air and water.

Their dedication and resilience made me feel all kinds of emotions—inspired, sad, angry, optimistic. And I became more convinced than ever just how important it was to fight climate change.

Then suddenly, the noise of the crowd subsided.

Being shorter than nearly everyone there that day, I stood on my tippy toes and tilted my head at various angles in an attempt to see what had caused the abrupt change.

"What's going on? Can you tell?"

"No," Mom said. "But clearly something is happening."

Uncle James took out his phone. He read a text message and then looked at us.

"Apparently some of the bosses and board members of Blackstone are here. They have agreed to meet with protest leaders."

"When?" Mom asked.

"I guess now!"

The crowd did not move. The chants resumed, but with increased vigor. They seemed to sense a possible breakthrough.

At just shy of four o'clock, I noticed something else. Hector and Tracey had been standing with some of their friends and family about twenty yards in front of us. Then the two of them started to move into the crowd. Why, I wondered? Was everything okay? Was *he* okay?

A half-hour or so later, they returned, and I dashed toward them, weaving through the crowd.

"Mia!" shouted Mom and Uncle James. "Hang on!"

Uncle James followed me. He was every bit as curious. Mom and Rebecca soon caught up.

"Is everything okay?" Uncle James asked Tracey.

"I think so," Tracey said.

"What happened?" I asked.

"They wanted to talk to Hector."

"Who did?" asked Uncle James.

"All these white guys in suits. The higher-ups from the refinery, I guess." She turned toward her son. "Tell them about it, Hector."

"They asked me about my asthma. About this letter I wrote to them around Christmas. About why I protest. About our housing complex that we had to leave. They asked if I can actually notice pollution when I'm home or at school. That kind of stuff."

"I guess one of the lawyers in the city, Ken Brown, suggested they talk to a kid," Tracey continued, "so they could understand better what it's like to live here, to grow up here. They said they would, and Ken mentioned Hector."

"What was it like, talking to them?" I asked.

"Weird. Super weird."

"Were you nervous?"

"Not really. At first, maybe. But then I was just telling them the truth. No tricky questions or nothing."

At about 5:30, one of those well-dressed men appeared beside the police. He borrowed a megaphone from an officer.

"We want you to know that we have heard you today," the man yelled. "We are going to continue to meet about this. You will hear from us in the next few days ..."

The rest of his words were drowned out by the

angry crowd. At first they summoned all of the energy and vocal power left in their bodies and booed, long and loud. Then the booing blended into "Let us breathe! Let us breathe! Let us breathe!"

I looked at Tracey, who was still standing near us and yelling as loudly as anyone. The anger was written all over her face.

Hector, on the other hand, didn't yell. He cried. The reaction from adults indicated that they had lost. He looked down at the pavement, and his shoulders heaved. He took off his glasses with his left hand and covered his eyes with his right. He cried like he had somehow let everyone down.

I should have consoled him, but I was paralyzed by confusion. The man said they heard the protesters. They'd talk about it. Wasn't that progress? Couldn't that lead to a positive outcome?

The crowd remained at full strength until close to six o'clock but then, gradually, people began to head home. With the police around, and so many children watching, they must have decided it wasn't worth fighting anymore that day.

I hugged Hector goodbye as he and Tracey got ready to leave.

"Maybe it'll be okay," I said softly to him. "Try to stay positive."

"Yeah," he said unconvincingly.

Uncle James led me, Mom, and Rebecca back to the elementary school to gather his belongings and get the car. As we started to drive away, I felt so unfulfilled. Was this it? Was it over? I needed some answers.

"Does this mean that they lost?" I asked Uncle James. "That nothing will change?"

He sighed. "I don't know. I can't say it looks good."

"But the guy said they'd talk about it."

"They always say stuff like that. Then they let some time pass and hope everyone forgets or moves on to other problems."

"But do they think the people will really forget? After all this?"

"I don't know. Maybe not. But if not forget, maybe give up."

"Do *you* think they'll give up?"

"No, I really don't. But there's only so much they can do. It's not their decision, unfortunately." He paused for a moment. "I just wish they didn't have to keep fighting anymore. They're not asking for much."

I didn't say anything else for a while. I was honestly crushed. It wasn't supposed to happen this way.

Chapter

"You've done everything you could," Uncle James told us as we prepared to board the train to return home. "You should feel proud. And it's not over anyway. There may be more for you to do."

I nodded. But I felt nearly hopeless. It was Wednesday night, three days since the protest, and there had been no news. In this case, no news felt like bad news. Like Uncle James had suggested, maybe the polluters were hoping the people of East City would give up and move on to some other injustice facing them. Or just back to their regular, busy lives.

"And remember," he added, "whether we win or lose this one, there will be many more battles ahead. Don't let this beat you up."

Well, I felt beaten up. Two days earlier, Uncle James had shown us a YouTube video of a Blackstone executive who had been briefly interviewed on the way to his car. The executive, clearly agitated by the surprise questioning from the reporter, expressed defiance more than sympathy.

"Yeah, we're aware of the size of the protest," he said. "And that was really cute. But reality requires that we focus on our job of fueling the entire country."

"He doesn't care about fueling anything," Uncle James had said with disgust when he played the video for us. "He cares about making money. It's what they all care about."

I hugged Uncle James before climbing aboard the train, and he held onto me a little longer than normal. Then he turned to leave Union Station as we somberly settled into our seats for a long trip home.

The past few days had actually been a lot of fun, despite the disappointment of the protest. I now undeniably loved Chicago, and I reveled in showing Rebecca some of my favorite spots from the September trip. We had enjoyed coffee—decaf with plenty of sugar for Rebecca and me—while peering out the coffee shop windows at all the interesting people as they passed by. We had walked to breakfast, lunch, and dinner, braving the cold. We even shivered our way through an ice cream cone on Tuesday night, not quite willing to call it a day.

Still, a pall hung over us throughout the visit. Uncle James would often check his phone, occasionally because I bugged him to, but by Wednesday morning, those phone checks had become less frequent. It had begun to feel futile.

When awake on the train ride home, Rebecca and I played games to pass the time, all the while chatting about school and our friends. Mom spent a fair amount of the train ride on her phone or computer, hunting for potential job opportunities.

I also exchanged a series of texts with Christian, informing him about the protests and answering his many questions. Multiple times, Rebecca looked at me and mouthed "BOY-FRIEND." I would squint my eyes and shoot her a disapproving look, but it would just make both of us giggle.

The train was scheduled to arrive in Boston at 1:30 on Thursday afternoon, and at 12:55, a phone rang. It was Uncle James calling Mom. She had been typing on it and accidentally declined the call, so she hurriedly called him back.

"Hey. What's up?" Mom asked.

She looked at us. "He wants me to put it on speaker."

"You all there?" Uncle James said.

"Yeah, we're here."

"All right, you're not gonna believe this. There's an article on the *Chicago Tribune* website today. They backed down! EurOil backed down! They agreed not to go ahead with the expansion! This is huge!"

Our smiles started small, due in part to disbelief, but then quickly widened. I looked at Mom and Rebecca, then back at the phone. "What? Are you serious? That's amazing!"

"Yes, it is! The EurOil people met with Blackstone board members, and it was decided that they didn't want all the negative publicity. I can't believe it!"

"See?" Rebecca said. "And you guys were all sad for nothing."

"Apparently!" said Uncle James, whose exuberance hadn't even slightly tapered off. "And get this. There's a quote from one of the board members. He said he was especially moved by hearing from one twelve-year-old boy."

"Hector!" I shouted, disrupting the peace and quiet of some disapproving nearby passengers.

"Exactly!" Uncle James said. "Can you believe that? The writer of the article also said EurOil didn't like the negative attention from the protest in East City, or others along the pipeline routes. And—ready for this?—the national attention this has gotten in recent months. They feared it could be bad for business and turn more people against fossil fuels, at a time when some people are really starting to pay more attention to this issue."

Mom looked pleasantly surprised and proud. "So, these girls may have really contributed?"

"They definitely did. You were both phenomenal. I hope you'll share this great news with your teachers and the other kids who were part of it."

"We will," I said, barely able to speak because I was so giddy.

"Mia will definitely share it with Christian," Rebecca said, grinning and looking up at me. I didn't even flinch.

"One more thing," Uncle James said. "We can't give up. This is a small victory. If EurOil is worried about negative publicity, then we need to keep fighting. Give them more to be worried about. I hope you girls are in."

"Definitely!" I exclaimed.

"We're so in!" Rebecca agreed.

"Great! I'll let you go. Enjoy the rest of your February vacations, girls. You deserve it!"

When Mom hung up the phone, I clenched both fists and tucked my arms tight against my torso, smiling ear to ear.

"I'm so happy," I said. "I feel like I want to scream!"

"Don't," Rebecca said. "I'm pretty sure that dude two rows over already wants to throw his orange juice at us."

"You must feel like you really accomplished something," Mom said. "Like all that hard work paid off."

"Yeah," I said. "And I'm so happy for Hector."

I then took out my phone to text Christian the good news. But I had signed up to receive climate-related alerts a few months earlier, and before I could message him, I was face-to-face with two news items:

"Scientists say last month was the hottest January on record."

"Wildfires continue to blaze out of control in Australia, causing animal and human deaths. Scientists blame climate change."

At that moment, Uncle James's words rang in my head. Sure, we had succeeded in East City after months of struggle. But that was one small victory in one city out of the entire world. The fight to bring the changing climate under control was far from over. It could be years, maybe decades, filled with victories and defeats. Oil companies still had gobs of money.

But I was ready for it. I did not intend to become complacent on the heels of one victory. After all, basketball teams don't earn a championship trophy after the first game of the season.

Chapter

The final day of February vacation was chilly and rainy, so I didn't even leave the house. I was determined to finish a book I had started in Chicago, and I also spent a good chunk of time texting with Christian.

That evening I sat at my desk with the Chromebook and wrote about our experiences in Chicago. I wanted to be able to tell Mr. Walker and Mrs. Young about it on Monday, and inform the Climate Club at our next meeting.

At one point, Mom knocked on my door.

"Come in," I said.

"Hey, enjoying some time alone?"

"I guess so. I missed my room. How's it going?"

"Well, I have some news," she said. "I just got off the phone with one of the editors at a website that reports on Massachusetts news. They want to interview me Wednesday for an opening."

"Yay! Congratulations, Mom! What's the job?"

"That's the really cool part," she said. "It's for an

environment reporter. I guess when the last reporter left, they decided to change the position to one that focuses on environmental issues in the state."

I started to smile, but then I summoned all the strength in my cheek muscles to resist.

"Wow, I thought you'd be happy," Mom said.

"Mom, I'm so happy that I want to jump up and start dancing," I said, the smile returning to my face. "I hope you get the job so bad, but I just don't want to jinx it."

"Ah, that makes sense."

"Good luck, Mom," I said. "And thanks again for last week."

"You're welcome, sweetie. I'm so glad we went."

I was up early the following morning, more eager than usual to return to school after a vacation, when a week of sleeping in can make it challenging to wake up for that first day back. So instead of exiting the house at 7:28, it was more like 7:15. I figured I could pass the time texting with Christian; his bus arrived earlier, so I assumed he'd be available.

But as I sauntered through my yard and into the street, I happened to notice Beth's car in Don's driveway. That was unusual for a weekday morning.

I glanced toward Don's house, and behind the storm door, the main front door was open, the first morning I had seen that in months. I tried to sneak a peek inside the house when, suddenly, a wheelchair rolled up to the door and into my view.

"Don?"

Don flashed a big smile, and he energetically waved to me. Instead of waving back, I rerouted myself toward his house, nearly jogging. Beth stepped around the wheelchair and opened the door for me.

I beamed as I entered the house. "Hey! Does this mean ..."

"No, not yet. But it might not be long."

"That's such great news!" I said as I turned toward Beth.

"It really is," Beth said. "I can't believe his progress. He's walking around with a walker now and doing so well. And the doctor says, based on his healing, he should be able to get around even better with a little more physical therapy."

Beth then looked at Don. "And then he'll have to keep up with the PT when he comes home."

"Yeah, I know, don't worry." He smiled at me and jokingly rolled his eyes. "Daughters. They can be tough."

"My parents would probably agree," I said.

"I had planned to come here today to take a look at how we can set up the house a little better for him," Beth said. "He begged me to tag along."

"I miss this place," Don said. Then, smiling at me, he asked, "So what have you been up to?"

I hardly knew where to begin, and I wasn't sure I should. I really only wanted to discuss Don's progress. But he encouraged me.

"I hear you went to Chicago?"

"Yeah! We protested against pollution. We wanted to support East City. This oil refinery wanted to bring in more tar sands oil from Canada."

"How'd it go?"

"So good! They actually decided not to. We were so surprised."

"I think East City was lucky to have you as their secret weapon."

"Oh, I don't know about that," I said sheepishly.

"They were so inspiring. They refused to give up. And they still face so much pollution there."

"Speaking of pollution, have you heard about those terrible fires in Australia?"

"Yeah."

"It's so sad," Don said. "I read that a lot of animals are dying. We've messed things up so bad that we're now causing fires that kill all these really interesting creatures."

I shook my head in disappointment. "I know."

"The world is gonna need people like you if they're gonna deal with this mess," he said.

I then glanced up at the article on the wall in his living room. Don's arrest. He noticed what I was eyeing. I looked back at him and could sense his pride.

"I'm really interested in hearing more about that," I said. "Could I come back sometime?"

"Well, you'll have to talk to my secretary," he joked. "But I'm pretty sure we can squeeze you in."

Beth laughed. "Oh, he'll have plenty of time for you, Mia."

Just then, we all heard the sound of the approaching school bus.

"I think that's for you," Don said.

"Yeah."

"Thanks for stopping by."

"I'm so glad I did."

I walked out the door and down the steps. As I got to the street, I turned around and glanced back at the door.

Don was still there, smiling. He waved to me.

I waved back.

Acknowledgments

I decided to write this book in the fall of 2019, and the COVID spring and summer of 2020 provided me with some extra time to produce the first draft. Naturally, it went through several rounds of edits before being published, and I am so grateful to those who gave their time and input to help make this book better.

My first editor was my daughter Rachel, who was ten at the time and within my target audience. That she didn't dislike my first draft was encouraging. When I changed the book to be directly from Mia's perspective, she read it again. She loves to read and, truth be told, has read more middle-grade novels than me (nonfiction is generally my preference). Her input was so valuable. My younger daughter, Samantha, has not read the book but she knows a fair amount about it, just from patiently listening to me talk about it so much. An avid reader herself, I'm sure it won't be long before she cracks it open.

My wonderful wife, Vanessa, read the full first draft and selected rewritten sections, and she graciously listened to me any time I needed to discuss the project. Perhaps most importantly, she didn't tell me I was in over my head when I floated the idea of writing it in the first place. My mom, Corinne, read two early drafts, and my dad, David, one. Their support helped to keep me going.

Two former colleagues, Tracy Duarte and Katie Plourde, both middle-school English teachers, generously read a draft and made helpful suggestions. Sirah Jarocki's feedback boosted my confidence and especially helped me polish the first ten chapters or so.

I'm so grateful to those at SDP for their support and enthusiasm for the book. Lisa Akoury-Ross was very understanding that I still have a day job that I love, and she made the process quite simple for me. And the book's editor, Cath Lauria, quickly gained my trust as someone who would improve the book while embracing my vision for it. She was a pleasure to work with.

I would be remiss if I didn't mention that without the work of journalists and scientists who have written extensively about climate change, I would never have developed the knowledge required to adequately write this book.

About the Author

Chris Casavant is a sixth-grade social studies teacher in Marshfield, Massachusetts. At his school, he runs a club for students who want to learn and act on climate-related issues. Before becoming a teacher, his career was in writing, first as a sports journalist and columnist, then as a writer in the business world.

Chris grew up in Dartmouth, Massachusetts. He received Bachelor's degrees in history and journalism from the University of Connecticut, and a Master's degree in history from Chicago State University. He lives in Plymouth, Massachusetts, with his wife Vanessa, who is a child psychologist, and his two daughters, Rachel and Samantha.

The Greatest Cause of Mia Dubois

Chris Casavant

Publisher: SDP Publishing

Also available in ebook format

www.SDPPublishing.com

Contact us at: info@SDPPublishing.com